BURIED

JUSTIN BOOTE

GET YOUR FREE BOOK!

GET YOUR FREE BOOK!

https://dl.bookfunnel.com/b00dfjcobx

ONE

Completely naked now, her clothes torn brutally from her, Amy Hunter grunted when something long and thick was thrust up her vagina and duct tape or something covering it to make sure it didn't fall out. It joined the other contraption someone had forced up her other hole.

"Get your fucking hands off me!" she screamed, her body coated in gashes and blood dripping from several orifices, several teeth missing. There were a few people dragging her but she had blood in her swollen, throbbing eyes and couldn't tell exactly who it was. Only Richard her ex-boyfriend and a couple of others. There had to be more though; she was being dragged by her long, black hair which had been torn off in places as she frantically tried to free herself, and others gripped her by her legs and arms. There was a torrent of punches and slaps, others hawking up great blobs of saliva and spitting into her face, although considering the amount of blood dripping down her, this didn't make much difference.

"You fuckin' whore. Think you can get away with fuckin' other people's husbands? Your *friend's* husbands, you little slut?

You gonna get what's comin' bitch and ya gonna suffer long and hard."

That was Richard. Behind his back because no one would ever dare to say it to his face they called him Deadbeat Dick. That was when he had a son of his own and bailed on the mother, refusing to pay child benefit. As far as they all knew, he hadn't seen his son since. The traitor. He had caused all this, incapable of accepting she didn't want to be with him anymore. And Richard took rejection bad. Resentment was what coursed through his veins instead of blood, revenge the adrenaline that kept him running. She should have known when she told him but even she couldn't have expected this much hate and violence. And now they were probably going to kill her or worse. Someone had dragged off her baby daughter before they pounced on her as well and this was killing her more than the beating she was currently receiving. If anything happened to her baby girl...

Was she watching right now as her mother was dragged along to God knows where? Screaming for them to leave her alone? She had no idea; she couldn't hear anything over the screams and yelling from those dragging her along the cold floor of her own house. Could she be dead too? The thought made Amy try harder to break free from her multiple restraints but all she achieved was for them to tighten their grip on her, deliver more punches to her face and chest. Someone gripped her nipple and twisted. Such was the pain she wondered if they'd managed to twist it right off.

She heard a door being slammed open and then a gust of wind on her battered face and knew she was outside. Probably the back garden with its high brick walls so no one could see in. It was a semi-detached house so she only had neighbours on the left-hand side and these were away on holiday for two weeks so they weren't going to help her either. She was doomed. If she thought her life had been shit up until now, practically forced to work as a stripper at that seedy shithole in town just to provide for her daughter, that was nothing compared to this. Amy landed hard on the garden from where they had thrown her. She could smell the grass and the rich odour of freshly dug soil as she landed face down. Someone kicked her hard in the stomach taking the little remaining wind from her lungs. People chuckled.

"Guess where you're goin', bitch? Right where the sun don't shine. Kinda fittin' you ask me. You'll be right at 'ome with all the maggots and worms. Maybe they'll start eatin' ya before you're dead. Wish I could stay to watch."

More laughter followed. It was that bitch whose husband had lied about her, saying Amy had tried to fuck him. It had been the three of them who orchestrated this little act of vengeance and when she was kicked into a deep hole, she knew finally what was coming. Panic invaded her. She had assumed they might beat her to within an inch of her life, leave her in hospital for a while as punishment, but not for a moment had she considered they would really kill her. Richard was an arsehole but he wasn't a murderer. What about Sam, her daughter? They were going to leave a poor, innocent girl without a mother? She'd already lost her father, who ran off when Amy told him she was pregnant. They couldn't. And not like this. If Richard wanted to be a real arsehole piece of shit, kick her to death until she felt no more and fell unconscious, but the hole she was lying in, scrabbling pathetically to find a way out from, no, not like this. It also occurred to her she was going to die in her most favourite spot ever, her garden, where she spent countless hours pottering about, experimenting with weird and exotic plants trying to make them grow in the frigid English weather. A huge cactus plant sat in the corner but its future looked as bleak as hers.

She heard a scraping sound and then something landed on her back. This process was repeated dozens of times and Amy tried to scream for help, beg them to stop but her vocal chords were shot from so much screaming. She tried to push herself to her feet yet every time she did so she was kicked back down again, chuckling and laughing all around her. It was starting to get heavy now, the pile on top of her. She could barely lift her legs and then soil began entering her mouth, ears and nose and she knew she had lost the battle. But the desire to survive, not leave her little baby all alone in the world to fend for herself gave rise to one last burst of frenzied resistance. Lying on her stomach she pushed herself up with both hands, the soil heavy on her and tried to climb up the sides. She fell down again when the shovel connected with the back of her head.

"See ya later, bitch. You deserve to rot down there with the worms, slut. Let's see ya fuck other people's husbands now. Hell's too good for whores like you."

The weight on Amy grew heavier, her breathing more laboured and within a few seconds the laughter above her faded away and her world went black.

Two

Summer must have come early was her first thought because it was still only May but she was extremely hot and sticky under the blanket. And contradictorily she had covered herself in the blanket as if it was freezing cold outside instead. Amy tried to kick off the blanket but it was stuck firm—she must have been really sweating during the night. Maybe she had a fever or something which was not good —who would take Sam to school?

It was practically impossible to breathe too, so much that she had a headache and only the tiniest amount of air reached her lungs, as though her throat and nose were filled with...

It hit her. She tried to sit up regardless but she was incapable, barely able to wriggle her fingers and toes. Then she tried to suck in enough air to scream, not just for help but because her own panic dictated this was the thing to do. Those fuckers had buried her alive but she wasn't dead. Not unless this was some grim version of hell anyway, but she could smell the soil covering her body and was vaguely aware of the sound of vehicles passing by, their engines distant in this makeshift grave. They had buried her alive and left her for dead, but somehow, miraculously, she was still alive. Barely, but alive. She didn't think she was now a ghost either or she could just float through the soil and appear above ground again. Whether she'd been unconscious for a matter of minutes or hours or days she had no idea; only that a God must indeed exist and had decided to keep her alive a little longer. Maybe He had a plan for her. But first to get out of here somehow.

Okay, keep calm. Don't panic. Breathe through your nose. If you're still alive it's because there's a pocket of air in here somewhere and it's keeping you going.

As she had begun to regain consciousness, she had been able to wiggle her fingers and toes. Now fully awake again, she noticed the rich smell of soil clogging to her nostrils, stronger than before and now she was vaguely aware of the soil being wet. Maybe it was her blood and sweat that had soaked the ground but she had more an idea that it must have rained heavily last night or this morning or whatever time of day it was and may have loosened some of the top soil. The weight on her back and head was certainly heavier but when she had lost consciousness there had been no way for her to move a thing—something had happened.

She wriggled her toes some more, trying to twist her ankles at the same time, while steadily doing the same with her fingers and wrists. It was almost like being buried in clay but gradually, by trying to be as patient as her broken mind would allow, she found she was able to move her digits with slightly more ease. She could almost bend her fingers now and her ankles wiggling side to side were gaining more traction. The urge to just try and push herself up with all her might was strong, very strong, almost impossible to resist, but she continued wiggling slowly —left, right, up, down, but always with an eye towards up. If she could successfully push away some of the soil directly on top of her, so the air would filter in through larger gaps. And her lungs were burning already now.

The struggle to keep calm was nearly as tough as pushing her way through the soil but she planted a picture of her smiling daughter in her head and told herself that if she didn't keep her act together that would be the only time she would be seeing her again. After being left for dead for God knew how long under here, all she needed was to panic, allow the wet soil to clog her nostrils further and really fuck things up. Finally, she could move her hands completely, curl them into fists, but she needed to keep bending her fingers back so she could curl them and scrape at the soil above her. She could wiggle her ankles completely now. She was also aware that she could really use a toilet and that was when she realised why her vagina and butt felt so cramped. *The fuckers. I swear I will get out of this and ram that fucking dildo down Richard's throat. As is.*

There was a slight movement above her. Suddenly, she was aware that her lungs weren't burning so much anymore, ready to explode in her chest. Something brushed across her eyelids and she almost screamed at that, believing Richard's prediction was going to come true, after all—eaten alive by worms. But then she felt it again and could have cried had her constricted chest and throat allowed. It wasn't some bug crawling across her face, but something she thought she would never feel again and it was gorgeous. Cold air on her face.

Her hands were almost bent back double as though she was trying to break her wrists on purpose, but it had worked. Slowly but surely, for what felt like hours but was probably minutes, her fingers had probed at the soil above her and had caused the soil to shift. She had to be on the verge.

And then it happened.

Her fingers poked through the tight confines of her prison and a cool breeze brushed over them. With renewed vigour, she pushed until her arm broke through like some giant worm getting its bearings. The utter darkness that had previously swallowed her whole was banished, replaced by the glorious beacon of daylight. Like a contortionist, she bent her wrist back and scraped at the soil above her, flickering it away until in one great surge of adrenaline, with her free arm she pushed herself against the weight above her and broke free. Sputtering and gasping she rose from her grim prison like some undead monster brought back to life again and rolled onto the grass beside her, inhaling as much oxygen as she could at once, burning her lungs again in the process.

I did it! I made it. I'm alive!

Amy rubbed the soil from her eyes and dared to open them. She had no idea how long she had been under there but the intensity of the sun upon her face almost blinded her, causing her to shield them from the bright light. And now that she was free and wasn't going to slowly die, a myriad of emotions and thoughts coursed through her. Her daughter, where was she? Water. She needed water badly or she was going to die of thirst instead. The toilet. And then she remembered what had been rammed up into her and she grimaced when she saw the duct tape crudely covering her parts. Oblivious to the pain, because she didn't think anything could ever be as scary and painful as being buried alive she tore off the tape and removed the dildos inside her. She looked at her naked body more thoroughly. Unaware of any bones broken but her body looked as though a pack of dogs had gone to work on her. There was barely an area of skin on her body that was its natural colour. Where the soil wasn't still sticking to her, the rest of her was a mash of dark bruises, gashes, scars and cuts. Her whole body ached, her eyeballs ached and she imagined her face was as bruised as the rest of her. Her tongue was swollen, probably from lack of fluids as well and when she ran it over her gums she was painfully aware of the gaps between her teeth.

She wanted to scream in delight for being free, jump up and run to Richard's house as she was—she didn't care—and stab that fucker right in the balls and watch him die instead.

But first she needed to know what they had done with her daughter and she needed hydrating. Amy pushed herself to her feet, immediately fell down again hard on the ground when her legs refused to obey and grunted. A white-hot bolt of agony ran straight through her bones causing them to rattle inside her. This time, taking more precautions, she pushed herself up slowly, stood there for a few seconds until she stopped swaying and the rush of blood to her head faded and took a tentative step towards her house. She was desperate to find out what had happened to her daughter, if they had hurt her in any way, but first she needed to get herself fixed. Sam would scream herself hoarse if she saw her mother like this but she didn't think she would be at home alone anyway. Richard was a fucker but he had never shown that part of himself around Sam, always treating her as though he was the father. Her guess was that Richard had probably taken her to his own home and had made up some story about Amy having gone away for a while.

Or maybe he hadn't.

As she glanced around the garden, revelling in the breeze on her skin, she noticed the cactus plant. It had been a mad idea of hers when drunk one day to buy it from the local gardening shop and try and grow the thing. She knew the chances were slim in the generally cold climate of England, but that was part of the challenge. It had grown to nearly four feet, covered in dangerous spines and she had often joked that any clients who failed to pay her for her services would find themselves tied naked to it. Richard and his cronies had moved it and left it directly above her grave. Now it sat there withered, drooping and half dead like her. The dildos that had been inside her were lying next to it and this gave her an interesting idea for when it came to seeking revenge. But that was for later.

Amy staggered to the back door, glad for once she didn't have any nosy neighbours wondering what the hell she was doing stark naked and covered in shit, and opened the door.

"Sam? Sam, are you here? It's Mum?"

No sound came from inside the house. Part of her expected Richard to come running, having taken over her house and the last thing he would be expecting was for his ex-girlfriend to have come back from the dead. It would have been so like him, kill Amy and keep her house, telling anyone who asked that she had left town for a while. Amy was well-known on this street; many of the neighbours had been clients of hers at some point while the wife was away. Anything to provide for Sam. Anything.

But no one came running, no one answered. Just in case, she headed upstairs and checked Sam's room. The fucker had taken all her toys and dolls with him, so this was a guarantee he planned on keeping her.

Sobbing, Amy went back downstairs and grabbed a bottle of water from the fridge. She drank it so fast she vomited most of it back up again, so forced herself to slow down, the cold liquid running down her throat the most wonderful thing on Earth. When they had left her no one had thought to turn off the electric or anything, so next, she headed into the living room and opened her laptop. It was Wednesday the thirteenth which meant she had been buried for almost twenty-four hours. Twenty-four hours buried alive, no one would have ever discovered her body because that fucking cactus plant was above her, so anyone looking would have assumed the freshly dug soil was to accommodate the plant. She might have decomposed, been eaten by the worms and bugs before anyone happened to find her body. The new neighbours after the rented house was finally reclaimed by the bank and wondered what the hell a dead cactus was doing in the garden. It was this thought, the realisation of how close she had come to dying, Sam left to fend for herself at such a young age that her grief and the horror of what she had been through finally caught up to her. She howled and sobbed for what seemed an eternity.

Once she got that out of her system, she was able to

compose herself better, think better. Her number one priority right now was finding out where her daughter was. She could call the police and tell them what happened but Richard, being the slimy, lucky fucker that he was would probably find a lawyer good enough to find him innocent. As soon as his lawyer started mentioning that Amy was a stripper at a seedy club, maybe even a few after-hours clients she took on to earn a little extra—and what kind of an example was that to show Sam?— he would turn the tables on her, perhaps even insinuate that she had deserved it, and Richard would be a free man. No, that wasn't going to happen. Richard was going to pay for what he did on her own terms. There was no way Richard would have taken Sam to Amy's mother or relatives either—questions might be asked. *Why hadn't Amy phoned us to tell us she was going away for a few days?* No, Richard would have kept Sam with him, and she knew the girl would be relatively well looked after. So that immediate sense of desperation could be banished too. Besides, she wasn't going anywhere looking like she'd just been beaten to death so the next step, and something that she really needed right now too was a scalding hot bath. Once she was cleaned up, then she could start to plan her immediate future. And that involved Richard Lenover and the other two who had helped him. A future that was going to involve lots of suffering and pain. More than they could even imagine. Being buried alive would seem like child's play by the time she finished with them.

THREE

From a very early age Amy knew she was different from other girls. She preferred playing with toy soldiers rather than dolls, creating vast armies then smashing them to smithereens with marbles that she would roll straight through the middle. From when she was about eight, she decided that she hated wearing dresses, throwing tantrums if her mother insisted upon her doing so. But eventually she got her own way, only having to wear them at special gatherings like Christmas or birthdays. She wanted her dark hair kept short, not long as she used to have it, and soon the majority of her friends were boys rather than girls. When she entered adolescence and preferred getting dirty with the other boys or playing football rather than netball, she realised she was a tomboy. Despite her mother trying to get her to look prettier by wearing makeup, she absolutely refused. So when it was time to start considering a career for herself, and not to waste too much time doing so because money was scarce in the house since her father ran off to younger pastures, it was welding that took her fancy. She had a friend whose father was a welder and she liked the idea of it. Working on the oil rigs out in the North Sea was her dream.

The amount of money they earned sounded like a dream come true if she could achieve that and then she could finally move out of this shitty town and away from her alcoholic mother and start to live life for real.

But she only got as far as doing a welding course then having to get a job as a waitress when money became even more scarce in the household. Amy never entirely gave up on her dream though. She bought a welding kit and in her spare time would practise in the back garden until she became pretty good at it. That same kit was sitting in her shed right now and she had an idea. A very good idea.

After she finished a long, hot bath and managed to dress the worst of her injuries, she had cried some more, drank nearly a whole bottle of wine and started considering her options. At some point she would need a dentist but that was later. In her current condition she wasn't going to return to work in a near future, and if things worked out bad she may never work again anyway. If things went wrong her near-death experience may become a permanent one next time. The important thing right now was that Richard and the others didn't know she had miraculously survived; only this way could she seek out her revenge on them and reclaim her daughter. And revenge was priority number one. She slept long and peacefully and this morning, despite her bones and muscles aching, she thought she was ready to put in motion her plans. Starting with the other two who had accompanied Richard—Jenny and her husband, Brian. It had been Jenny who Richard spoke to, telling her that Amy had been messing with her husband.

It was ironic how Amy ended up considering she had been a tomboy most of her life. When Sam was born her wage as a waitress didn't cut it, especially since the father disappeared as soon as the word 'daddy' was suggested, so she had to make ends meet another way. She had always had a perfect figure, pretty face and breasts large enough that most men's eyes drifted towards them rather than her face so when she was offered a job as an exotic dancer at the After Midnight Club she said yes. Now, for the first time in her life she was expected to wear makeup, wear not dresses to work but miniskirts, look sexy. She hated it but Sam needed feeding and babysitters didn't work for free. And as Sam grew larger and needed more toys and ate more, working as an exotic dancer wasn't cutting it either. It was when a regular to After Midnight, a guy she thought pretty cute anyway, suggested she might earn a little more doing even more than dancing on a stage, she ended up working three jobs and only two of them she paid taxes on. Within a few weeks, one regular client became several, each with their own demands and fantasies that they liked to play out with her. If it meant Sam not wanting for anything like had been the case with her, then she would do it. She hated herself for it, felt disgusted with herself and her body afterwards, but Sam was not going to have the life she had had.

It was for this reason Amy kept an assortment of sex toys in her drawer. Dildos, vibrators, of various sizes and colours, according to each client's needs. She had three regulars who liked to watch her fuck herself with them beforehand, while getting in the mood. She also had another regular who was married but harboured a secret—he was bisexual but could in no way reveal his secret to anyone. So, instead of risking being caught with another man, he preferred Amy to do the work. She pulled out the ten-inch strap-on from the drawer and held it up. This thing had been up the guy's arse so many times its pink colour was starting to fade. It was a heavy thing, made from thick rubber and she needed two hands to insert it properly into the client. She wouldn't have dared use the thing on herself and she had been with some big guys.

Amy took it out to the shed where her welding kit was passing the dying cactus plant on the way. "Sorry, big boy. I'll try harder next time, I promise."

In just a couple of hours her weapon of choice was ready. Her whole body shook with nerves, not too dissimilar to when she had realised what her mode of death was going to be two days ago, but she took a couple of shots of whiskey, reminded herself what they had done to her and why she was doing this and headed off towards the home of Jenny and Brian Sinclair.

She didn't have an exact plan and was hoping the element of surprise would be a major factor. After all, it wasn't every day you buried someone alive and they actually came back to haunt you, so hopefully this would give her the time she needed to at least subdue them, assuming both were at home. If not, she would wait; she had all the time in the world right now. Just in case though, her largest kitchen knife sat in her bag along with her other toys.

The only idea she had in her mind was to casually walk up the garden path and knock on the door. Those precious few seconds as Jenny or Brian glared at her in shock and horror would be enough to barge her way in, perhaps administer a quick cut to the face or something to let them know she meant business. Her heart throbbing in her throat, part of her telling her to just run away, that this was madness and find Sam, she knocked on the door before she could change her mind. Her heart sank as she stood there for what seemed like ages and no one came to the door. They were out, she was going to have to go through this all again, if she had the nerve to do so, but then she saw movement through the glass panel. Her hand tightened around the knife now up her sleeve.

The door opened and as predicted Jenny stood there, her jaw dropped, eyes wide and bulging as though seeing a ghost. She made no attempt to slam the door shut again, as if she was paralysed. Amy grinned.

"Hello, Jenny. Didn't expect to see me again, did you?"

"Y-You. You're dead."

"And so are you."

Amy quickly let the blade drop from her sleeve and in one deft swipe, opened Jenny's cheek. This brought Jenny back to her senses. She tried to slam the door closed, but Amy had been prepared for that and her foot was in the way, preventing it. She pushed her way in and slammed it shut herself. Jenny tried to run but Amy had that covered too and grabbed her long dark hair and viciously pulled her back before putting the blade against her throat.

"You ain't going anywhere. Is Brian home as well? Make my life easier, two birds with one stone and all that."

"No, but he will be any moment. Then you'll be sorry, bitch. You should have stayed where you were. Once Brian finds you, you're gonna regret coming for us. You're a sick fucking woman. You don't deserve to live."

Amy cut a line across Jenny's throat, not enough to cause serious injury but just enough for her to know she was serious. She dragged the woman upstairs to her bedroom and threw her on the bed, keeping the knife firmly against her throat at all times.

"Where's Sam? Has Richard got her? If he so much as touches her..."

Jenny, despite the trail of blood running down her chest and the fear in her eyes suddenly looked at Amy as though she had gone mad.

"What are you talking about, Amy? Are you still carrying on with that crap?"

"Don't you fucking lie to me! Don't you fucking dare! I know Richard has her and I'm going to get her back. You fuckers, all of you."

With the knife handle she bashed Jenny in the side of the head as hard as she could sending her reeling back onto the bed. Amy put her bag down and took out a roll of duct tape. She straddled Jenny and put her hands above her head, then before her old friend could react, tied her wrists to the headrest. She then did the same with her ankles, tightening them as tight as possible. When Jenny regained something of her senses and tried to scream for help, another strip went across her mouth.

"You ain't going nowhere, girl. And I know you're lying about my Sam. I'll get her back. They took her from me before, and I got her back."

Jenny thrashed her head from side to side.

"Yeah, you deny it all you like. Besides, I didn't come here to talk about that. I came here for you. Was it your idea to put my cactus plant above my grave? Or was it Richard's? Either way it doesn't matter."

From the large rucksack she produced her new toy and showed it to Jenny. Jenny thrashed and writhed on the bed, eyes virtually popping from their sockets.

"Was it you put the dildos up me? I bet that was you. Kind of thing a dirty little slut would think of. Payback is a bitch, bitch."

With the knife she cut away Jenny's dress, then her underwear leaving her naked.

"Cute body, Jenny. No wonder Brian wanted nothing to do with me. Not that I tried anything, anyway. It was all a lie, Jenny, did you know that? Richard lied. I bet Brian fucks you real good, don't he? I bet you beg for more. Well, I'm gonna give you more. Much more."

The strap-on in her hand was getting heavy now. She stepped into it and tied it tight so it didn't droop. Amy was proud of her work and by the look in Jenny's eyes, she had every right to be. Around the huge rubber toy and then the tip, Amy had bent a thin sheet of aluminium, then welded tiny steel needles to it barely a millimetre long. It resembled a mini cactus plant.

She climbed onto the bed and lifted Jenny's legs in the air. She thrashed as hard as possible, wriggling like a giant worm, her muscles taut, veins standing out, eyes ready to fly from their sockets.

"No good struggling, Jenny. Didn't do me any good either, did it? When I catch Brian I'm going to do the same to him too, then Richard then take back my baby girl. Bye, Jenny, I hope Hell is warm enough for you."

Knowing it would have been hard work at the best of times, Amy grabbed a jar of Vaseline she had brought with her and coated the strap-on careful not to cut herself on the deadly protuberances. Slowly she pushed it into Jenny's vagina, just the tip.

Jenny's face was bright red now, muffled screams coming from her taped mouth, her head rocking violently as the strap-on was slowly introduced.

"How's that feel, Jenny? Feel good? Like having your pussy filled, right?"

Tears of agony ran down Jenny's face but Amy hadn't even got started yet. Slowly she pulled it out, then back in until she built up a nice rhythm. Already blood was beginning to form underneath the struggling woman as the sharp needles raked and tore at the walls of her vagina. Then Amy started to build up speed. Just as those cheating fuckers did to her she built up speed thrusting harder, pretty sure she could hear the walls of Jenny's vagina tearing. The blood came thicker and faster, a sticky, crimson mess soaking the bedsheets. Then, when Jenny's face looked like it might explode, so bulging and red was it, she introduced all ten inches of the sex toy. With the extra layer of aluminium, the thing was nearly as thick as her wrist but thanks to the Vaseline it slid in easy. The blood gave it that extra bit of lubrication too which helped. She rocked back and forth, imagining—or at least trying—what it must be like to have the insides of one's vagina ripped apart as though someone had forced their hand in and were scraping at the sides with long, sharp fingernails.

It was hard work by now but she continued rocking back and forth, knowing now why men tended to sweat heavily while in the throes of sex. She should have brought a bottle of water with her, she realised, as she pumped away. The bedsheet beneath her was really soaking now, so much blood that a puddle was forming, too thick to soak through the thin fabric. Jenny looked like she was on the verge of blacking out so she gave one good thrust as hard as she could causing Jenny to smash her head on the headrest behind her. That brought her back.

Then she had another idea. The thought of being left for dead, to die slowly, while they probably spat on her makeshift grave and laughed, slapping each other on the back. *Great job, guys. A job well done. Let's go celebrate.* She could quite happily let Jenny bleed to death, her insides ruptured, but she wanted more. Besides, she was curious. She'd had some pretty big dicks inside her over the years and always wondered how far up they reached. Now would be a good time to find out exactly how far.

Amy grabbed her knife again and inserted it into Jenny's stomach straight through the flesh and began to saw. With renewed strength Jenny struggled, writhing, trying to kick Amy off her but it did no good. Then Amy began to saw a circle just below her bellybutton. Once she finished she threw it on the floor and peered in the hole. It was amazing. She could see the strap-on in there and it had definitely ruptured some organ straight through the middle. A liver maybe or kidney? Who knew. She continued fucking Jenny almost hypnotised by the sight of her sex toy pounding away up and down. If Jenny had been pregnant, well, she wouldn't be anymore. The inside of her stomach was a pool of blood and swimming tissue and organs that had been sliced off. Jenny groaned.

Sensing the end was near and Amy really needed a drink now as well, maybe a shower now that her legs were covered in Jenny's blood, she pulled out the strap-on, straddled Jenny's chest and beat her face with the toy, rubbing it across her cheeks and lips, destroying those too. As a final touch, she then ran it hard across her closed eyes, tearing off the eyelids. Jenny's eyes looked up at her almost pleadingly, but it didn't matter—Jenny was dead.

But still Amy wasn't finished.

She wanted a trophy. She had an idea that she had been thinking about since yesterday, and really, the garden did need tidying up. She thought it would be a fitting tribute to what they had put her through. With the knife, now sticky and less sharp than before, she began to saw away at Jenny's throat until she reached the tough cartilage. Then she dragged Jenny's body until her head was hanging over the side of the bed and began to stamp it, as though trying to snap a thick branch. Eventually, the cartilage broke and with one final kick, Jenny's head dropped to the floor. Whistling to herself, Amy put the head in her rucksack along with all her other materials and headed off home. It was a nice day—perfect for a spot of gardening.

Four

"Come on, you love it. Bit of kinky never hurt anyone. I bet ya done it loads of times before."

Richard held up the steel handcuffs and dangled them before Amy's eyes. She had already kitted herself out in her sexiest gear that he liked her to wear—pink stockings and suspenders, high heels and a white, lace bodysuit. And while she wasn't averse to a little kinky shit as he liked to put it, the idea of being tied to the bed, defenceless, was something that made her a little nervous. Richard could get a little carried away sometimes, to the point it got a bit painful even. He was already half drunk.

"I dunno, Richard. I'm tired. Why don't we just fuck like we normally do? Maybe another day? I was up most of last night with other clients and my bones needs a rest!"

"For fuck's sake. Why do ya keep doin' that? Workin' as a hooker? You'll get pregnant or some fuckin' disease. Ya don't need to do that anymore."

"Yes, I do. I don't get paid enough being a stripper. And I need the money. We both do, me and—"

"Stop, don't start that again. We've been through all that already. Now, you gonna put on the fuckin' handcuffs or I gotta do it my way?"

Damm it, she wasn't going to be able to talk her way out of this one. And she wasn't lying; the guys she'd screwed last night must have been on speed or coke or something because they'd been banging away at her for what seemed like hours. All she could do was tell herself it was for Sam.

"All right, but not too tight, okay?"

A big childish grin appeared on Richard's thin face. His light brown hair tied back in a ponytail, scrawny arms and skinny body he didn't look the kind of guy who could hurt too many people but once he got going, his strength seemed abnormal. Richard grabbed both her wrists, threw her on the bed, then handcuffed her wrists to the bars on the bedrest. He pulled off the Metallica t-shirt and scruffy jeans leaving his cock erect and throbbing in anticipation then tore off her knickers and roughly spread her legs, then seemed to decide against it and put her ankles up behind her ears.

"There, see. Now ain't that cute?!

Amy thought she looked a bit stupid. Ten years ago she would never have envisioned herself wearing all this slutty crap. She looked like a dressed-up Barbie doll. But, despite his occasional bursts of anger and the way his eyes would flare up, looking like he was gonna beat the living shit out of her, she guessed she did love him in her own way. Either that or she was just glad to have someone to take reasonable care of her. And Sam loved being with him and it seemed the feeling was mutual. She just had to save up enough money until she could get out of this area and start again. If Richard wanted to handcuff her to the bed now and again while he fucked, it was hardly a big deal. Some of the things her clients did to her were nothing compared to this.

She grunted as he entered her—no foreplay with Richard—

and mentally pictured Sam smiling in her head so she had some-thing good to focus on. At the speed and force with which Richard was fucking her, he wouldn't take too long anyway. And that was a good thing—her vagina was aching today; it needed a break like the rest of her.

As predicted Richard soon finished and flopped down on the bed beside her.

"So, umm, you wanna get me out of these handcuffs? My wrists ache."

"What? Oh, yeah."

He untied her and Amy flexed her arms trying to get the blood rushing back into them. She was ready to fall asleep already when Richard sat up and stared at her with a weird look in his eye—a way she had never seen before. And was he blushing?

"So, umm, Amy, I was thinkin'."

"That why you look so stressed?"

The look in his eyes momentarily disappeared, replaced by another she knew well. But it was just a brief instance and then it was gone again.

"Haha, very funny. Look, now that things are kinda normal again and you're much better now, I was thinkin' like, what if we got married?"

All sleepiness was torn from Amy's body. She bolted upright as if she'd just seen a huge spider in bed with them. She stared at him, hoping, praying, he was joking.

He wasn't.

"What? Don't look at me like that. I mean, we could live together and save money on two rents. That way ya don't have to work as a hooker anymore. Works for both of us."

Then he pulled out a ring from his trousers pocket on the floor and held it up. "So will ya? Marry me?"

Amy's mind was reeling. Yes, financially it would make sense, but what about Sam? Sam was away at a relative's for a while and what if she didn't want to? What if, once they were all living together, Richard would then have more of a hold over her, and she would be trapped under his roof. Because there was no denying that he would fully expect her to live here and not at her place. Sure, working as a part-time prostitute would be over and thank God for that, but to marry the guy she only hung out with because it was one of the very few who had never shunned her? Only a day ago she had been thinking about saving money and getting away from this shitty town and everyone in it. She couldn't do it.

"Richard, I...Listen, you know I like you. A lot, I really do, but...I don't wanna get married. Not now. Not to you not to anyone. I really appreciate the offer though, honestly, but...sorry."

Wanting to avoid his gaze she looked down at her hands and saw they were trembling. She could almost hear Richard's blood boiling in his veins, feel his eyes boring into hers. A quick glance told her what she suspected; his hands were curling into fists. Richard did not take rejection lightly. She dared to look him in the eyes. He slapped her across the face.

———

"SHE'S A BITCH. A FUCKIN' whore who fucks anything. She'd fuck a dog if she thought it might pay her. Like that guy they caught who liked fucking with dogs. I'm tellin' ya, Jenny. She's been tryin' it on with Brian, I saw her."

Richard watched the change of expression on Jenny's face. From disbelief to anger, her lips curling upwards, eyes beginning to bulge, turn red. It was working. It had taken him weeks to first save the money for the stupid ring in the first place (which he had considered stealing from the old man at the jewellers) then to build up the courage to ask her. Now that she appeared to have got over her issues with Sam, it seemed the perfect time. And she had practically laughed in his face. She had probably told everyone she knew already by now and they were having a good laugh at his expense. Richard the romantic. Richard going soft in his old age. Yeah? Wrong, bitches. She was going to pay for rejecting him. She was going to suffer.

"And you saw this?" asked Jenny finally as they sat on her sofa drinking a beer each.

"I'm tellin' ya. They were in the pub and she could barely keep her hands off him. He kept tryin' to keep her back—it was obvious he wasn't interested, so don't go takin' it out on Brian —but I heard her too. Come back to my place. I'll show ya a few things, that kinda thing. She's a fuckin' slut and don't give a shit about no one. Shoulda fuckin' stayed in the hospital."

"I'll kill her," said Jenny softly, and without any emotion in her voice.

Richard grinned. "I think somethin' needs to be done about her. She's like this parasite, preyin' on everyone's husbands. Before ya know it, all you women gonna be divorced or got some sexual disease because of her."

Richard thought he could almost see the cogs spinning in her head, considering her options. Several years previously, Jenny had spent three months in prison for assault on another woman who had tried this very thing Richard was suggesting about Amy. Jenny had broken the woman's leg, arm, and left her with severe concussion, so with this girl, anything was possible. It was why he had gone to her.

"Where is she now?"

"At home I guess."

"Okay, well when Brian comes home I'm going to ask him about it, what she said, and if so, Amy's in a lot of trouble. I'll fucking kill her myself. Brian is mine."

Later that night after discussing it with her husband, Jenny had then phoned Richard to tell him her plan. That bitch wasn't going to go around fucking with anyone's husband anymore. The only fucking she would be doing by the time they'd finished with her would be in hell. And she thought the best place to carry out her little act of vengeance would be in that stupid garden of hers with that stupid cactus plant in the corner like some hideous, alien monstrosity.

FIVE

Brian's job as a long-distance lorry driver meant he was away from home for extended spells. Sometimes a day, sometimes a few days and this particular one meant he had been gone for just over twenty-four hours, a journey to Scotland so he had decided to stay overnight. She knew because she had returned to Jenny's house, hid what was left of the body —or more to the point, kicked it under the bed—then changed the bedsheets, took Jenny's mobile phone and returned home again. She had pretended to be Jenny when he texted her and when he phoned she texted back to say she had a sore throat. But the important thing was that she knew the exact time when he'd be arriving home. He'd even texted asking if there was news about that bitch Amy. She'd had to stop and giggle at that one for a moment. Oh yes, there was lots of news. One could lose their head over so much news.

And in the next half hour or so, Brian was due home. Amy hid in the wardrobe of their bedroom, her trusty rucksack beside her, knife up her sleeve. He would expect to find Jenny in bed this late at night so would come running up the stairs, barge into the bedroom and stop when he saw she wasn't there. And when he saw the little spots of blood dotted about that Amy purposefully hadn't cleaned, he might start to panic and that was when she would pounce. Catch him unawares.

As before, her mind was trying to give her a thousand reasons to just back out now, go home and forget about it. She'd got away with it once, this time she might not be so lucky. Brian wasn't the biggest guy in the world but, like Richard, he was still a hell of a lot stronger than she was. All it needed was for something to go wrong, miss with the knife and she was going to die herself. Again. Then the back door opened and any thoughts of calling it all off vanished along with her nerves. It was time to get to work.

"Hey, Jenn, I'm home!"

Amy listened as he slammed the door shut and was no doubt rushing about the house looking for his wife. Amy suppressed another giggle. In a way she kind of wished Sam was here to see what was coming—she might find it funny as well.

"Jenn? Where are you? I'm back!"

Then she heard the footsteps on the stairs as he dashed upstairs, surely excited to get his hands on her again. Like most men, sex seemed to be about the only thing he ever thought about. Sex, beer and football. In whatever order. The guy should probably shower a bit more often though. Amy had often heard women giggling about him in the room, saying he smelled like goat's cheese. Gross. Amy didn't want to imagine how potent that smell might be where he kept the business end of things.

She was convinced he would be able to hear her heart thundering in her chest when he walked into the bedroom but instead, as she peered between the slits in the wardrobe door, he was more interested in why the bed was empty and where his wife was. The last text Amy had written suggested she would be in bed waiting for him in very little clothing.

"Jenn? Where are you? This some kind of game?"

Amy let the knife slide down her sleeve. The timing was crucial. One wrong move and she would never be seeing Sam ever again. Or anyone.

"I get it. Hide and seek, is it? I can play that."

Amy's heart dropped. She hadn't planned for being caught in the tight confines of the wardrobe where she could barely move, let alone swing a knife. With the amount of movement she currently had she would barely graze his skin let alone cut his throat open. Then she exhaled softly when she saw him get on his hands and knees to look under the bed.

"Dunno what you've been doing, Jenn, but smells fucking nasty down here. You been pissi..."

Brian gave a combination of a whimper and a squeal as he jumped back banging his head on the corner of the bed. This was the moment she had been waiting for. Amy pushed open the wardrobe door with Brian helpless and his back to her, surely incapable of understanding what he was seeing and quickly went to him, putting the blade against his throat.

"Slightest move, I cut your throat open."

Brian flinched but did as he was told. "Who is this? What the fuck is that thing under my bed? Some kinda animal?"

"I think you know the answer already to both of those questions, don't you?"

Brian's muscles visibly tensed. "Th-that's impossible. You're dead."

"So's your wife. Her head is sitting on my mantelpiece. I fucked her hard with a strap-on just how she likes it then I cut her head off. How do you feel about that? Do you feel the same sadness as when you buried me alive? I don't suppose you do, do you, which is a shame."

She could tell he was considering his options, ready to lash out at any second. She could see his hands already curling into fists. Wouldn't do her any good to play with him. There would be plenty of time to play when he was safely bound and gagged.

But first he needed subduing. She stabbed him through the cheek so the blade came out the other side.

While he groaned and tried to scream—instead gargling out blood—she kicked him onto his stomach and handcuffed his hands behind his back, the same cuffs Richard had used that fateful night. Then she rolled him over. He looked very funny with that knife through his face, as though he was grinning. But his eyes suggested otherwise.

"Didn't do a very good job, did you, Brian? I was nearly twenty-four hours buried alive in my own garden. Do you think I really deserved that? Tell me, whose actual idea was it to bury me alive? Was it Richard's, Jenny's, yours? I'm guessing yours or Jenny's. I just don't see Richard being that imaginative and constructive. I don't suppose you know where my daughter Sam is, do you? I think she's with Richard but I'm not sure— I'll go find her tomorrow maybe once things have settled down."

Brian was trying to say something but it was evidently complicated with a knife stabbed through his face.

"Sorry, Brian, didn't catch that. Shall we remove the knife so we can hear what you got to say for yourself?"

He shook his head vehemently causing the blade to catch on the tiled floor thus injuring himself further.

"Fuck it." She pulled it out anyway.

Brian howled in agony.

"What were you saying, Brian? Didn't understand you the first time."

"You fuckin' bitch," he managed.

"That the best you got? I'd really love to know why you all decided to do this to me. What did I do? I remember Jenny saying something about me hitting on you. Is that what it was? Because it's not true and you know it. My guess is that Richard didn't like me rejecting his marriage proposal and he got upset. Did he tell you he proposed marriage and I said no? I bet he didn't. So then you all cooked up this little plan to get back at me. Well you fucked up, didn't you? Once I've taken care of you, I'm going to do the same to Richard and rescue Sam and we're getting out of here."

"What are you talking about? You're fucking sick. You know that? They should never have let you out. You're delusional, that's what. Sam is not—"

"Uh-huh, that's enough of that. You're the ones that are sick. Jenny's pretty fucking sick right now. Off her head with sickness!"

Amy burst out laughing.

Brian momentarily forgot he might be bleeding to death and tried to kick her from his position on the floor, only missing her ankles by inches. That reminded her she wasn't entirely safe from his clutches yet. Time to get a move on before his desperation and panic got the better of him.

Amy picked up the knife and wiped the blood off on Brian's chest, while considering her next course of action. She wanted him to suffer prolonged bouts of agony just like Jenny had done but she really had no desires to undress him, see his hairy arse then fuck it with her strap-on, which was sitting in her rucksack. It had occurred to her though, which was why she had brought it with her. But no, thinking about it some more, and while it sure would be fun, she didn't think she had the stomach to do so. Maybe Richard; she'd seen his hairy arse enough times.

What she had also brought with her was one of her gardening tools. She had already decided that it would be fitting if Brian and Richard died in a way that was related to her garden, since that was where they had buried her—her precious, beloved garden. She had considered bringing her rake with her but for practical purposes it wasn't designed too well for what she had in mind so instead she had brought another—in this case, perfect. Amy went and fetched it from inside the wardrobe and when Brian saw it, he began to writhe and struggle harder, trying to wriggle away like a maggot, lashing out at her with his legs. She really should have tied them together, she realised. Too late now though.

Amy raised the garden fork and brought it down hard on his balls. At least that was where she was aiming for, right in the middle with the four prongs so she at least stabbed something. A satisfying tearing sound followed as the prongs went straight through the man's flesh. Brian bolted upright in a reflex action then back down again hard, screaming in agony which in turn caused the gashes in his cheeks to open further, filling his mouth with fresh blood. Amy struggled to pull out the fork, wiggling it from side to side and when she did, there were small, fleshy lumps attached to two prongs that might have been his balls, cock, who knew?

A fresh pool of blood formed beneath him, then even faster when she repeated the action, aiming just slightly to the left to ensure she didn't miss anything. Brian, almost unconscious by now, groaned.

"See, Brian, this is what happens when you fuck with the wrong people. You don't ever get to fuck again. I'm going to cut your dick off now and put it in your wife's mouth that is sitting on my mantelpiece with the rest of her head. A marriage made in Heaven, wouldn't you say?"

She took out her knife and sliced through the thick material of his jeans, revealing his now semi-mutilated dick and balls. In one deft slice his flaccid cock came off and she put it in her rucksack. She was getting bored now, so figured it was time to finish the job as she intended. Amy stood up, raised the garden fork high above her head and brought it down repeatedly on Brian's throat. It jabbed into the tiled floor beneath, as jets of blood streamed into the air and rained down on Brian's face. Such was her fury that she missed at one point and stabbed the fork straight through his mouth, shattering his teeth, embedding it deep in the back of his mouth. With both hands she managed to retrieve the tool and for good measure thrust it into the centre of his head so it punctured both eyeballs. They came out stuck to the prongs like punctured golf balls. With her foot she kicked them off.

Not quite finished, she stabbed his throat several more times with the garden fork, using one foot to turn his head first to the left, then to the right, inflicting as much damage as she could. By now she was tired and thirsty, so grabbed her trusty knife and sawed through what was left of his neck. Which wasn't a lot. His head came off finally, the sound like someone tearing off a leg from a plump chicken. She put the head in her rucksack and gave one last look back at who used to be her friend before leaving with her tools. She prayed no one spotted her with the fork covered in blood. She really should have brought a spare set of clothes as well, she scolded herself as she left. Maybe next time.

SIX

As she headed home, feeling somewhat satisfied that her job was nearly done, yet still sad it had come to this, Amy contemplated how it was possible for some people to be so cruel. Just because she had turned down Richard's proposal, declined to marry the man. As if she was the last woman on Earth condemning Richard to a life of solitude and celibacy. He was probably fucking someone else already, Amy forgotten about. He'd probably forgotten he'd even helped bury her alive, living with Sam and pretending that her mother had gone away for a long time abandoning the pair of them. How could such cruelty exist still? It was like living in Medieval times again—she was surprised they hadn't crucified her instead.

Had she gone a little too far when it came to dishing out revenge? No, she didn't think she had. For years, since an incident she couldn't recall anymore, they'd been calling her sick, mad, that she should be locked up in Northgate the rest of her life, but that wasn't fair. Sam had had...issues. All Amy had done had been try to help her. She was Sam's mother; it was her duty. Sam was innocent, she had nothing to do with any of this and now the poor girl was probably crying herself to sleep each night wondering why her mother had disappeared again. For that alone, Jenny and Brian deserved everything they got and in Richard's case, was to come.

Tears forming in her eyes, she hurried past the local park on her way home, the rucksack heavy with the strap-on and now Brian's head in there. It was late which meant unless someone walked right next to her they would be unlikely to see the blood splatter on her body but she wanted to get home quick regardless. It wouldn't do to get arrested or stopped by the police before she dealt with Richard. That would be disastrous. But as she rushed past she heard familiar voices in the park, laughter, which caused her to stop and listen. She thought she heard her name mentioned a few times too, and was that a young girl she could hear giggling?

Her heart froze in her chest. That was Sam's giggling—she'd recognise it anywhere. What the hell was she doing out here this late with these people? She had school tomorrow. For a second she thought of rushing over to them and asking them what they were doing until she remembered the state she was in and that she was carrying a bloody garden fork. Instead, she crept closer and hid behind a brick wall. There were four of them there, Richard included, plus Sam, the four adults drinking beer as they sat on a park bench while Sam played alone on some swings, out of ear reach.

"Can you imagine dyin' with a dildo stuck up your arse, man? They say when a person dies they piss and shit 'emselves. You reckon she shitted the dildo out squeezin' too hard?"

More laughter followed, belching and the crushing of beer cans, followed by others being opened.

"Shoulda stuck one down her fucking throat as well, choke her on it. She was used to it, after all. Couldn't keep her hands, mouth or pussy away from someone else's cock," said a woman. "I really wanted to see her face as she breathed her last breath. Be the last thing she ever saw before going to hell."

That was Kate. Kate had been a co-worker at After Midnight. They'd been good friends. Or so Amy thought. But the thing that was running through her mind now was maybe it wasn't just Jenny, Brian and Richard who had buried her. Had these others participated as well? She tried to recall but it was all so blurry. She had been at home with Sam. There had been a knock on the door and the next thing she knew she was lying on the floor, her head as though someone had cracked it open with a hammer. She had been aware of blood, dull aches to various parts of her body and insults hurled at her as she lay there. Then she had been vaguely aware of being carried upstairs, laughing and joking, more insults, someone punching her on the vagina. Her clothes torn off and something that she later knew to be two of her dildos roughly shoved up inside her all the way. But yes, now that she thought about it, there had been more than three voices. At least two women. Jenny had a husky voice, almost like a man whereas Kate's was squeaky like a little girl.

"Richard, come and push me!" called Sam from the swings. The others ignored her. Amy's heart dropped.

She dared to peer from behind the wall. There was Richard with Kate and her husband, Donald. She'd been a witness at their wedding. And there, with his big, fat gut, was her ex-boss, Charlie, from After Midnight. Ex-boss because she was supposedly dead and Charlie wouldn't be expecting her back anytime soon. So he had been in on it as well. All orchestrating her death behind her back and now they were laughing and joking about it while Sam innocently played alone right nearby. Amy was thinking that maybe it might be time for After Midnight to die as well—all its employees and its fat owner maybe burn to death. Like that movie, Carrie, she could lock them all in and set fire to it, listen to *their* muffled screams for help.

Barely aware that she was crying, she listened to them laugh at her further, wanting nothing more than to run to her daughter, snatch her up and run away, perhaps stab Richard with the garden fork at the same time. And she was very close to doing so too, having to forcefully will her legs to stay put. She wasn't going to do anything with just a kitchen knife, a strap-on resembling a cactus and a fork. But oh those fuckers, they were going to pay.

"You reckon the maggots and worms've started on 'er yet?"

"She's such a slut they probably don't even want to touch her. Might get poisoned or something from her fucking blood."

"Has anyone seen Jenny or Brian? I've been texting Jenny the last couple of days and she isn't answering."

"Brian just got back from work, I think. You won't be seeing those two for a while. Probably fucking right now as we speak! I'll phone her tomorrow."

"Look how high I am, everyone!" called Sam. Again, they ignored her.

Amy watched Sam swinging back and forth, a grin on her face as though everything was fine with the world and this broke Amy's heart too. She should be crying, begging to know why Mummy had left her, yet at the same time, she was also glad to see that Sam was being treated okay, even if she did have school tomorrow and it was late. But for now, there was nothing Amy could do except go home, deposit Brian's head and plan for this unexpected twist. Just when she thought she only had Richard left to deal with, her schedule just increased dramatically.

SEVEN

Richard was not the kind of person to scare easily. In fact, the only time he had ever been truly scared was when he beat up another kid at school when he was ten and the teacher decided to phone his parents. It had been the third time that week Richard had beat up another kid and the headmaster had had enough. The only reason the headmaster hadn't phoned his parents before was because he knew what Richard's dad was like. And he was right. Richard arrived home early from school after being suspended to find his father waiting for him with his leather belt in his hand. Richard had been unable to sit down properly for several days afterwards, had been unable to sleep properly for four nights and his father told him that the next time he got sent home from school for fighting, he'd never be able to sit down again. Richard believed him.

His father had been a total fucker but the man had principles and so did Richard. When it came to his friends and their wellbeing, he was first in line to help out wherever necessary. Unless they fucked with him, of course, like Amy had done, rejecting his marriage proposal just to hurt him. She often did things like that, sometimes without even realising, which was partly why they had been forced to have her sent away for a spell. But right now, it wasn't exactly fear that was tugging at Richard's nerves, more unease, but the two sensations were closely related to each other. Unease was not a part of Richard's chemistry either.

And the reason for this unease was because he had been calling both Jenny's and Brian's phone since yesterday and neither were answering. There was always the possibility they were copying Lennon and Ono by hiding in bed for twenty-four hours, getting all cuddly with each other, but not for this long. He'd left about a dozen messages on each one's phone and they would have seen them by now and responded. Jenny was *always* on her phone. This told Richard that something was wrong. Very wrong. For one not to answer their messages was feasible, but both? Nope.

Yet the funniest thing that kept replaying through his head, as though it was him that needed a lengthy session at Northgate and not Amy, was an image of precisely her. Only a few days ago it had been Jenny who wanted to make Amy pay for trying to seduce her husband and Brian had been all for making sure she paid properly for what she did. Originally, her idea had been bury Amy in her stupid garden for a little while, perhaps give her the tiniest access to oxygen so she didn't die—a thin tube perhaps—then let her out later. Let her know that if she did it again the next time there would be no tube and she would be staying there. But before they carried out their little plan, with the help of the others Richard had told, Jenny had needed something for her nerves, just so she didn't bottle it at the last moment and she had been half drunk. That changed every-thing. Then, thoughts of giving Amy a little tube to breathe through had been replaced by "fuck her, she's a slut anyway and is never gonna change so let's do it right."

That had made Richard a tiny bit nervous. Now they

weren't going to just give the woman a bit of a scare but fucking kill her. If they were caught that was life imprisonment and Richard wasn't so sure he was capable of that. He might have to go and kill himself as well—he'd heard some nasty stories about what went on in Norwich prison. Playing the soap game with the inmates. But if he backed out now, especially after it had been him that started all this off in the first place, they would call him a coward. He'd be branded for life and that was almost as bad. He had a reputation to live up to, one that had taken years to cultivate. Just like that exotic crap in Amy's garden.

Now though, as he headed towards Jenny's house, the idea that kept trying to latch onto the forefront of his mind and stay there, was the possibility that somehow Amy had managed to escape after all and was seeking a little revenge of her own.

"Bullshit," he muttered. "There's no fuckin' way she got out."

He'd filled the soil in himself, making sure to press down the soil firmly so she couldn't fumble her way out again. That hole had been deep. Well, pretty deep because it had been hard work digging it and he was tired by the time it got to filling it in again. He had asked if Brian or Donald wouldn't mind giving a fucking hand but they had spouted some crap about it being symbolic that he did it, her being his ex-girlfriend and all and he'd had no choice. So no, there was no way she had managed to dig her way out unless she had come back as a fucking zombie or something and not even she was bitch enough to do that, so there was a very good reason for Jenny and Brian not answering their phones. Too busy screwing all day and night, that was all. And Jenny was pretty hot, so yeah, he could understand that. He'd fuck her himself if given the chance.

He arrived at their house. Nothing looked suspicious, no front door wide open splattered in blood, so he walked down the path and knocked on the door. When no one came to answer he knocked harder. Had they gone out for the day? It was possible, but what wasn't possible was that they didn't send him a single text to say they were okay. Brian had told him he'd phone Richard the day after returning from Scotland to go for a beer and it was now well into the afternoon and still nothing. Richard knocked even harder, then pulled out his phone and tried again while peering in the living room window.

And that was when the first suspicions of something terribly wrong filtered through. A bottle of wine lay on the carpeted floor, its contents having spilled out looking like blood. Jenny would fucking kill Brian if he did that.

He tried the front door and it opened so he poked his head in and called to them. That he received no answer made him even more nervous. If Jennifer was on the toilet it was one of life's guarantees that her phone would have been with her. His muscles taut, as though preparing himself for a fight, he checked the bottom of the house and picked up the empty bottle, setting it back down on the table. The wine on the carpet was now dry. Alarm bells rang in his ears.

"Brian? Jenny?" he called.

There was no indication of a fight, nothing to suggest burglars. The TV was there, Jenny's laptop sat on a coffee table. He headed upstairs. A whiff of something foul drifted up his nostrils. Richard checked the bathroom, then moved to the spare bedroom and then, at the back, the main bedroom. The smell was stronger here and this put Richard on full alert. His hands curled into fists, he kicked the door open that was slightly ajar and waited for someone to come running at him. When no one did, he took a tentative step inside. He wasn't entirely sure what he was expecting to find—the possibilities were many— but the small splatter of blood on the far wall was a good indication he wasn't wrong in his assumptions. But as far as he could tell neither Jenny nor Brian were here. The smell was bad though. Didn't they have a cat? Maybe it had died in here because it fucking smelled like it. And there was a buzzing sound that was driving him crazy too that he couldn't locate the source of.

As he entered further into the room, he saw the blood stain on the floor on the other side of the bed and knew his suspicions had been proven correct. Something bad had happened to them but where the fuck were they? That stain on the floor, now dry, was big. Very big. It occurred to him that the smell was coming from under the bed. Richard got on his hands and knees and lifted the blanket to check underneath, fully prepared to be welcomed by the sight of a decomposing cat.

He screamed.

It was more from unexpected shock than a full realisation of what he was looking at because at first he wasn't entirely sure. It looked like some mangled animal carcass under there, too big to be a cat or dog though. The thing was a misshaped bundle, totally covered in blood, and it was only when he saw the arms and legs he understood what he was seeing. And even then, if it wasn't for the mutilated vagina and the breasts he would have been hard pressed to determine if it was Jenny or Brian. Without a head it wasn't easy. And for a brief, terrifying moment he thought she was still alive too because she appeared to be moving. It was then he realised she was covered in flies squirming all over her body.

Richard jumped up as if he'd been bitten and almost crashed to the floor again on unsteady legs. It was then he happened to peer over the other side of the bed and saw the decapitated remains of Brian, his body also covered in dried blood and massive puncture wounds around the groin and top of his chest. A swarm of flies rose into the air, the buzzing a horrible sound that grated in his head.

Richard turned and vomited on the floor.

He considered himself a tough guy but the sight of his two decapitated friends was too much even for him. He staggered from the room, not sure where he was going or what he was going to do. Phone the police, yes, that was a good idea, but then he remembered he'd just thrown up in there and well, his police records weren't exactly the cleanest so they might want to ask him a few more questions than usual. But he couldn't just leave them there either. Not like that, left to rot like roadkill. No, he was going to have to phone the police. He had alibis. If he didn't phone them, someone would come looking for them at some point, the police would be called, forensics would find his DNA in the vomit and he'd be fucked. There was also the thought that somehow the police might make some kind of a connection to these two and the missing Amy Hunter. Which, in turn, would lead to connecting him.

And that nagging doubt he had been having on his way here returned with a vengeance. Some fucker had brutally murdered his two friends. Who and why would someone do such a thing? A list of names ran through his mind. Those they may have gotten into fights with, arguments, but not a single name occurred to him. They were good people. Brian worked hard, Jenny a proud housewife. When they weren't burying people alive, of course, but that was different. Therefore, the only name that kept coming back to him like a possessed boomerang was Amy.

"Did you do this, Amy?" he asked out loud. "You come back from the dead or somethin'?"

A few times since killing her, Richard had taken it upon himself to revisit the scene of the crime. Not just out of curiosity, ensure that no one had found the makeshift grave and dug her up, but also because he liked to sit and ponder his actions. It gave him a hardon to think that she was under all that earth, never to be seen again, imagining what condition her body might be in by now. Had the worms started on her already? Probably. But now, he thought he might have to revisit once again for a different reason. An image of going to the back garden, opening the gate and finding a great hole there with no body, was one that was giving him considerable torment and grief. It was surely impossible but he had to know. After he had checked, phone the police and tell them the truth; he hadn't heard from his friends for a couple of days and had been worried. Nothing to connect him to their deaths or Amy at all. Richard quickly left the premises and headed towards Amy's house. But then he had another idea. Instead of phoning the police, it might be better to go and tell Kate and Donald what he had seen first. Just in case.

EIGHT

He had barely dare look but when Richard arrived at Amy's, headed around to the back garden and peered in, there was no giant, empty hole, nothing to suggest Amy was anywhere other than where she should be —in it. He was pretty sure the cactus plant had been left directly on her grave but he could have been wrong about that. He had more pressing things to think about anyway. From there he went straight to Kate and Donald's home.

Both were unemployed and spent most of their day and money smoking dope and snorting whatever they could get their hands on and listening to seventies rock so when he heard the music blaring from their living room window, any ideas of finding them dead as well were banished. He knocked on the door and long-haired hippy Donald came and answered. The couple both looked like peace-loving hippies but they were both temperamental characters. Years of coke and alcohol had ensured a faulty wiring in their brains, which was why Richard had had no qualms telling them about Amy screwing half the town behind his back. They had been more than willing to help him out.

"Hey, man. What's happening?"

"We need to talk. Serious shit, Donald. Can I come in?"

"What? Sure, man. Come in. Nothing too serious I hope?"

"Yes, it is."

Donald said no more and let him in. The living room was thick with pungent smoke, the culprit between Kate's lips.

"Hey, Richard. How's it going?" she asked.

Even though Kate was in her late forties, Richard had always fancied her with her long blonde hair that almost reached her waist, big tits and piercing green eyes. He'd fantasised a lot about fucking her, and there was something about the way her gaze always lingered a second longer than normal on him suggested the feeling was reciprocal. But Donald was bigger than Richard—much bigger—and he would fucking kill him easily. Richard wasn't that stupid to risk it.

"They're dead."

He didn't know how else to say it or where to begin. Richard still couldn't believe it himself anyway. That stench still lingered in his nostrils and the sight of his two decapitated friends would haunt him for weeks.

"Who's dead, Richard? Don't leave us guessing like that," said Kate.

"Brian and Jenny. I just came from their house. Someone fuckin' decapitated 'em."

"What?" they both cried in unison.

"Is this some sort of morbid joke, man, 'cause it ain't funny?"

Richard shook his head. "I can still fuckin' smell 'em. They're both in their bedroom, been lyin' there a couple of days I reckon. They're covered in flies."

"Holy fuck. Have you phoned the police? Who could have done that to them? And why?" asked Kate.

"I dunno. And no, I haven't phoned the police yet. I had this weird vibe like, like maybe it was Amy or somethin', somehow escaped and wanted some revenge. So I went to her house and checked the garden, but she's still there. But I threw up on their floor so when the police do come they're gonna get my DNA so yeah, I gotta phone 'em. But fuck man, their heads are fuckin' missin'. Someone took 'em."

"You thought *Amy* did this, man? What the fuck? Amy's dead. We buried her alive. She ain't going nowhere except hell. And yeah, you better phone the police before someone else finds their bodies or you're gonna be suspect number one when they do a DNA test. Shit, I can't believe it. Who could do such a thing, man? They were cool people."

"I know. So yeah, I just wanted to make sure you two were okay as well, before phoning. It just seemed a real weird coincidence, that a few days after doin' what we did to Amy, two of those involved are found fuckin' decapitated. I had to check. Maybe she dug her way out or somethin'."

"Yeah, right. And now she's come back as a fucking zombie. Get a grip, Richard. They must have made enemies somehow. Maybe they owed money for dope or something. Something Brian was up to while away and they found where he lived."

Kate was right. He had allowed his imagination to run wild. But hell, after seeing his two friends dead in that manner, he figured he had a right to start thinking weird shit was going on. Even so, despite knowing they were right and it was just a coincidence, he decided he was going to be keeping an eye out from now on, just in case. He could easily acquire a gun from one of the guys down the pub and now might be a good time to start carrying it around with him, hide it under his pillow at night when asleep.

"Listen, do you want us to come with you, when you call the police? 'cause they'll expect you to be present to give a statement. They are probably gonna list you as their number one suspect for a while too. That's what they do, man, so you better behave for a while, no going back to Amy's house and checking in on her fucking garden. They must be looking for her by now anyway."

"Okay, yeah, that'd be cool. Just in case they wanna fuckin' arrest me or somethin'. The last couple of nights I've been down the pub and I got alibis. And they ain't gonna find no fuckin heads in my house anyway."

"Come on, then, let's go, man."

Richard really didn't want to have to deal with the police under any circumstances, especially when there was a double murder, but he knew he had no choice. Donald would make sure he got a lawyer if necessary—he was good at stuff like that. Donald kissed Kate and together the two of them headed back to Jenny's place to phone the police.

———

AMY, who had first followed Richard to their home, then sneaked in the back door and eavesdropped the whole conversation, smiled as Richard and Donald left.

NINE

With what the police were going to find at Jenny's place, Donald and Richard were going to be gone a long time. Amy had been fully prepared to take on Donald and Kate at once, but now things were perfect. Almost too perfect. And when Donald did finally return home he was in for one hell of a shock. As soon as the two men left, Amy crept upstairs to what she assumed was a spare bedroom and took off her rucksack. The thing was damn heavy and she groaned as she dumped it on the bed. She really should have gone to the gym when she was younger, but then, she didn't know she would be carrying heavy, metal strap-on's with her everywhere. Not to mention her enemy's heads. The two she had at home were really blossoming well now.

Even though she had been a witness at their wedding, she had never been best of friends with Donald and Kate. She had known as soon as she met Richard he had a thing for Kate, the way he couldn't keep his eyes off her arse or tits was an instant giveaway, so she had tried to distance herself from her. Except when they were all at the pub then she made damn sure she kept herself close to Kate. But of course, back then she had believed herself to be in love with Richard, or at least a variation of it. Now, they could go fuck themselves and each other as much as they liked. In hell, of course. And so, because of that, she rarely came here when invited—jealousy might have been an issue, as well—so wasn't too sure of Kate's routine. Maybe she liked to have a nap after lunch which was about now, so the idea of waiting for her to fall asleep then waking her rudely sounded fun, but either way, she couldn't risk hanging around for too long in case Donald came back while she was hard at work so quickly took off her clothes and dumped them on the bed.

Amy took out the strap-on and carefully stepped into it, again careful not to cut herself. Cleaning the thing had been a real pain and there was always the chance she could get infected if she managed to graze herself. When she had planned on how to kill Brian and Jenny, she had taken into consideration the fact they had accused her of trying to seduce Brian so naturally it had to be his balls she cut off. With Jenny, it had been the fact that she was the real slut between the two, hence practically fuck her to death. It seemed fair. But with Kate, what little she did know about her was that she was one hell of a gossiping bitch who couldn't wait to start spreading rumours around the village, and even better if a scandal came as a result. Amy had the perfect plan for Kate. Donald was another matter, but now it seemed he would have to wait until later.

In the straps holding up her sex toy, she placed the kitchen knife she'd used on Brian and Jenny, again careful not to cut herself having sharpened it last night and debated whether to wait a little while or get the job done now.

She decided on the latter. Besides, the strap-on made her back ache, stupid thing dangling there like some obscene torture device, which, of course, it was.

Amy quietly and calmly headed downstairs, where she heard Kate chuckling over some programme she was watching on TV, no doubt stoned out of her brain which would make her job easier too. Amy was slightly bigger than Kate as well, who at nearly fifty, would have totally lost any speed and reflexes to fight back. This was going to be easy. She stepped into the living room and stood there, saying nothing. Kate didn't even seem aware of her presence.

"Hello, bitch. Do I look pleased to see you or what?"

Kate almost fell off the sofa in her surprise. She stared at Amy as if she couldn't believe what she was seeing—a zombie come back from the dead. She rubbed her eyes, perhaps assuming she was hallucinating from the potent weed she was smoking. And then her eyes happened upon the strap-on and her eyes widened even more—bloodshot and bulging.

"I...I'm dreaming. Imagining things. You're not real. That's not real. I fell asleep on the sofa and I'm dreaming this. I want to wake up."

She sounded like a little girl having a nightmare. Amy walked up to her, took out the knife and slashed the blade across her face.

"That'll wake you up, then. Bitch."

It took a few seconds for that to register as well. It was only when Kate touched her cheek and her hand came away covered in blood, that Amy could almost see the scream bubbling at the back of Kate's throat. But before she had time to release it, with both hands she grabbed the strap-on and swung it at Kate's mouth, smashing her lips open, the bottom one so badly cut it was almost torn off. But before Kate could react, Amy grabbed her around the throat and threw her to the floor. The blood was already pouring down Kate's chest, soaking her Pink Floyd t-shirt while Amy quickly took out her duct tape and bound Kate's wrists. She then did the same to her ankles, before cutting through the t-shirt and her skirt leaving her in just her underwear.

"Didn't expect to ever see me again, did you? What was your involvement in all this, huh? Richard tell you I was fucking your husband behind your back or you just enjoy burying people alive, you sick fuck?"

Kate shook her head and tried to say something but it was difficult having two mouths. Instead, blood bubbles formed between her destroyed lips which then broke sending crimson saliva everywhere.

"You always did have a big mouth, didn't you? Just had to spread shit about others, causing shit all the time. And you call yourself a fucking hippy. Did you think about my Sam while you were burying me? Did you make her watch?"

When Kate shook her head again, Amy sliced off her nipples. Kate coughed, showering Amy in blood splatter again. Amy was barely aware of it, focusing only on glaring into Kate's eyes, looking for any suggestion of remorse or guilt. Instead, all she saw was death. But she couldn't die yet, Amy hadn't finished with her by a long shot.

She had brought a little extra something this time too. A little experiment. When she discovered the other day that both Donald and Kate were involved it had hurt her badly. To think so many people could get together and plan such a gruesome, cruel death. If they had thrown her in front of a bus, or shot her, thrown her from the upstairs window, to kill her instantly was one thing, but a slow, agonising death? Nope, they had to pay and pay well for that.

With Kate's previously green eyes now bloodshot and red, staring up at Amy in what might have been pity or agony or both, she pulled out a little bottle and unscrewed the cap. Gently holding one eyelid up, Amy poured a little bleach onto her eyeball. She'd read somewhere about some serial killer doing so to one of his victims and that it was painful as fuck and judging by Kate's reaction, it was true. She might have been on the verge of falling unconscious or even dying but her body suddenly started flipping as if undergoing an epileptic fit. She opened her mouth to scream, having obviously forgotten about the gash to her cheeks and the now missing lips and inadvertently tore open her face even more as she tried to scream. Ignoring her, Amy did the same to her other eyeball then carefully used the kitchen knife to slice off the eyelids for good.

"See no evil."

She poured the rest of the bleach into her ears, having no idea if it was as painful or not.

"Hear no evil, and the best is yet to come, Katie, dear."

Acutely aware that Donald could return at any moment, it was time for the finale. The strap-on almost forgotten about while she played with the bleach, she grabbed it and gently eased it into Kate's mouth.

"There, speak no evil too. I bet you always did enjoy sucking dick, didn't you? Anyone's for that matter, you little whore."

There was a ripping sound as Amy slowly moved her hips back and forth, more blood pouring from Kate's mouth and the open gash on her cheeks. The gash opened further as she guided the contraption in and out of her mouth, to the point she could see it inside her, just as she had with Brian. After a few seconds of this, Kate's mouth had widened to the point her cheeks had been torn open so her mouth formed a giant O, her cheeks flapping and rippling as the strap-on moved back and forth. Kate's jaws and gums were now visible, teeth stained red, gums ripped to shreds. But Amy was getting bored now so decided it was time to say goodbye. Looking Kate directly in the eyes which by now appeared to be melting from the bleach poured onto them, she straddled the woman and pushed all ten inches of the sex toy into Kate's mouth, feeling the tip hit the back of her throat and force itself further down.

"Now that's a deepthroat, huh!"

Amy grabbed the back of Kate's head and moved it up and down, just as so many men had done to her, forcing her to deepthroat them. Kate struggled feebly, face a deep shade of red that wasn't just blood. Kate's tongue was torn to pieces, little globules stuck to the toy until it came away entirely. Teeth were also stuck to it as the sharp protuberances brushed past her gums. And then, Amy brought Kate's head up until what remained of her face was touching Amy's groin. They might have been playing some lesbian game had anyone been watching from the living room window. Amy left her this way until she stopped struggling and her arms flopped back down. Three down, three more to go.

As before, Amy picked up the kitchen knife and began to saw through Kate's head. It was hard work for some reason, so she stood up, took off the strap-on and started smashing it against Kate's throat, as though trying to knock her head off with a baseball bat. This was even harder work, so she resumed slicing with the knife. Eventually, sweating by now with the exertion, there was an audible tearing sound and her head came away. Another fine job completed. Amy considered hanging around for Donald but by now she was tired and hungry so threw the head into her rucksack along with her other tools, headed upstairs to get dressed again, and headed off home. But despite being happy with her day's work she was crying as she did so. She really missed Sam and didn't know how much longer she could hold out.

TEN

As Amy tended to her garden, her heart burned with the fact that she hadn't seen Sam in over a week. What was she doing? Was she crying herself to sleep each night wanting to know why her mother had abandoned her again? Was Richard treating her well? He always had before, so she had to assume he was now. Would Sam forgive her for having left her a few days? And could Amy ever tell her the real reasons why she had been away this time? What would she say if Amy told her that Richard and a few others, who had always treated Sam as if she was theirs, had buried her alive? Left her to die asphyxiated? The poor girl would be traumatised for life, knowing that such cruelties existed in this day and age. She might tell her friends at school and then they would all think of Amy as a witch, come back from the dead. A zombie. And given what she had done to some of those that had caused such a despicable act, they might not be so far from the truth.

The police were involved now too. Would they find her DNA and come kicking her door in? She hoped not, she thought she'd been very careful about that. But if they did find a fibre or something she was going to prison forever. Probably

Northgate Hospital for the Criminally Insane and no one ever left that place alive. It would mean she would never see Sam again. Just the thought made Amy drop her gardening tools, sit down on the soil and cry her heart out for all the injustices of the world. It also made her recall the last time she had been in hospital, Northgate Hospital for the Mentally Impaired.

The nurse, Catherine, the one who seemed to treat Amy with the most sympathy, came in one morning with Amy's medication.

"Morning, Amy, how are you feeling today?"

"Much better, thanks! So, I was wondering when I can go home? I really miss Sam and I know she's not allowed to come here, but I really want to see her again. I'm sure she misses me too."

Catherine frowned. "Come on, Amy, don't start all that again. If you talk like that you'll never get better and be allowed to leave."

"But what are you talking about? Don't you think it's normal for a mother to want to see her daughter? You have two children as well. How would they feel if you suddenly disappeared for weeks at a time?"

"It's completely different, Amy. If you don't take your medication, you can't go. We all make mistakes in life and Sam would understand completely that mothers are not immune to making them as well. But if you don't stop making it hard for yourself, they won't let you leave. I'm sure Sam is happy right now and you need to accept that."

"Of course, she's not happy! She misses her mother! How can you say that?"

But Catherine said nothing and ignored her; instead handing her the pills she needed to take each morning. It frustrated Amy immensely that they lied to her like this, telling her things they thought she might want to hear when all she wanted was to go home. Yes, she'd made a mistake but she was better now. Nothing bad had come of it, not really, and she had been here for two weeks now. She was fine! She would go home, speak with Sam about it, and Sam would understand. If only they let her go!

Later that day, Jenny and Richard had come to visit her, looking a little nervous, probably not sure what to expect. The last time anyone had visited she had gone apeshit when told she couldn't speak to Sam on the phone and had been restrained by the nurses.

"Hi, Amy, how's it goin'?"

Jenny only smiled and sat down.

"Hi, folks. I was speaking to the nurse earlier, asking her when I could go home, but they still won't let me. I told her I'm fine now, I don't need to be taking their medication but they still won't let me go. It's so frustrating!"

"Yeah, well maybe a couple days longer or somethin'. No point rushin' stuff."

"Rushing? Sam is waiting for me at home and you tell me not to rush? How is she by the way? Is she okay? Does she ask for me? Does she remember anything about what happened?"

"Amy...look, uh..."

"Uh, what? Just tell me Sam is okay."

"Yeah, she's fine. Asking about you all the time. I, uh, told her you were okay, comin' home soon."

"Richard," interrupted Jenny. "I don't think—"

"You don't think what?" yelled Amy. "What would you know, anyway? You don't even have any kids. You could never understand!"

"Richard, I think we should leave. I—"

"When are you going to let me speak to Sam on the phone, Richard? You promised!"

Amy jumped up from her chair to confront her boyfriend. Stupid idiot was red in the face, not looking her in the eye. They were all against her, every one of them, conspiring against her and she had had enough.

"Okay, we gotta go. We'll come back next week," said Richard.

"Don't you dare leave without telling me how Sam is! You better let me speak to her on the phone tonight or I swear I'll... I'll."

She tried to punch him, claw his face with her long finger-nails, but he was too strong for her. He pushed her back onto her bed and together the two of them hurriedly left. He was probably fucking her as well, the cheating arsehole. If only she could escape, get back home...

But then the doctors had come running and sedated her again, and she knew no more that day. It had been another month before they finally let her go home.

Amy wiped her eyes and looked around. It wasn't going to happen again. They weren't going to take her away again. Not to Northgate or prison. She'd kill herself first. Better that than Sam seeing her in a psych ward or locked up with criminals. But that wasn't going to happen either. Tomorrow, she was going to take care of Richard, claim back her daughter and get out of this town, start fresh, and forget any of this had ever happened.

Eleven

The outcome had been as expected. After seeing the condition of the two bodies, several officers had run from the house to throw up in the garden and had then frantically called for forensics and backup. Neither Richard nor Donald could blame them and despite being the enemy, actually felt a little sorry for them. When Donald had insisted on seeing the remains for himself, he had thrown up too.

Then, of course, the questioning had begun when the lead detective arrived and the carnage was confirmed. He had wanted to take Richard down to the station immediately but through Donald who had more experience in dealing with detectives, he had given a statement to an officer and agreed to visit the station later. The look in the detective's eyes though—and which had caused Donald to insist on visiting later while accompanied if necessary—suggested Richard might be at the station for more than a couple of hours. He might, in fact, be spending all night there once they checked Richard's record. It had only been when Richard told him that if he had committed those crimes, he would have cleaned up the vomit himself and left, saying nothing. The bodies were already beginning to rot, especially Jenny, so why would he inform the police? If he was lucky, in a week's time the bodies would be unrecognisable and there would be no DNA or anything on them. Reluctantly, the detective let them go, but insisted he pay a visit to the station later that day. Richard guessed that once they checked his police records, they would come knocking on his door instead. But that was for later.

"So who do you think did it?" asked Donald as they headed back to his place. "That looked personal, man. People don't decapitate others unless it's personal or it's some serial killer psycho."

"I dunno. Like I said, my first thought was Amy somehow escaped and did it, but fuck, I even went to her garden and checked. She's still buried there. I reckon Brian got into shit while away, drug dealers or somethin' and they wanted payin'."

"Dunno, man, but whoever it was, I hope they catch them quick. Some nasty shit went on in there, poor folks."

They arrived at Donald's and stepped inside, both having agreed that a stiff drink was required and quickly. They could both smell the stench of decomposition still.

"Hey, babe!" called Donald. "You are not gonna fucking believe what happened to Brian and Jen...Oh no! Oh fucking hell, no!"

Richard rushed into the living room after hearing Donald screaming and stopped. It took him several seconds to realise what he was looking at despite seeing practically the same thing an hour earlier. But it seemed impossible, it wasn't happening. His head was all fucked up and he was imagining shit. Mainly because the same thoughts were now running through his head as that morning. Except now, they refused to go away and he knew instinctively they weren't going to either. One image took centre stage in his mind. An impossibility, something that had no right being there but there could be no denying the obvious.

They had fucked up, big time, and now, one by one they were paying the price for it.

Donald turned to Richard, disbelief and horror in his eyes, and as though he could read his thoughts, knew what Donald was thinking too. This was no angry drug dealer or unknown serial killer stalking the streets. It was the work of a woman who should be buried several feet below ground. How the fuck had she managed to escape before dying from lack of oxygen? *She didn't, that's what,* he told himself. There was another explanation, one as equally fucked-up, but it had to be the answer.

Richard's mother had fancied herself as a bit of a psychic back in the day, reading people's palms and such, and apparently she had quite a reputation. Friends would visit her when loved ones died and she would try and contact them. According to local legend she had quite a high success rate. Richard and his father especially thought it was all bullshit but he didn't seem to mind the extra few pennies that sometimes came into the household. When Richard was a teenager, she had told Richard several stories of ghostly visitations, namely Richard's grandmother after she died. He had never believed her, of course.

"She's come back, Donald. I'm fuckin' tellin' ya. Amy's come back as a fuckin' ghost and is gonna kill us all. That or a zombie 'cause I'm pretty sure ghosts can't actually touch anyone. Maybe a vampire or somethin'. We gotta do somethin' to stop her or we're fucked."

Donald looked like he might hit Richard at any moment. He glared at him for a long time. Did he think Richard was joking? At a time like this? He'd never been so serious in his life. Right now, he was fucking terrified about waking up in the middle of the night and some ghoul standing over his bed about to tear his head off. Because that was obviously what had happened to Kate. What was left of her neck looked like it had been torn or bitten off. Lumps of flesh and skin were dotted around the floor that was covered in Kate's drying blood as though a pack of dogs had been fighting over the best bits. The smell was sickening.

"Are you joking with me right now? What the fuck are you talking about?"

Richard glanced down at Donald's hands and saw they were curling into fists. Unless he defused this situation fast, he may end up headless like Donald's wife.

"No, I'm not jokin'. Amy's dead, right? Yet of the six of us who buried her, three are now dead. What does that tell ya? There's no way she dug herself out alive—I checked the garden today—so she's fuckin' come back to haunt and kill us. Get revenge. First, Brian and Jenny, now Kate. And what are the police gonna say? Bit of a coincidence, right? They're gonna think we did it!"

Donald's arms dropped by his side. His shoulders slumped, tears ran from bloodshot eyes. Richard breathed a sigh of relief.

"So how do we stop her, man? She killed Kate, man! Fucking decapitated her!"

"We gotta dig her up and do the same to her. Then burn her or somethin'. I saw films like that as a kid. That's always how they killed the monster—cut off their head then burn 'em."

"But what do we do about Kate? I can't just leave her here, man. We got to phone the police, but what do we say?"

"First, let's go take care of that bitch before she comes for us as well. Then we'll think of somethin' afterwards."

"Right, man. Yeah. Fuck. *Fuck*, my poor Kate, man. She was everything. I can't live without her, man!"

"Unless we do somethin' about Amy, you won't have to. C'mon, let's go."

They arrived at Amy's, cast a quick glance around to make sure no one was watching the house or anything—detectives, perhaps, in their now paranoid state—and hurried around to the back. Things looked a little different than before but Richard didn't have time to worry about that now. Maybe

Amy's spirit or whatever she was liked to do a little gardening too; Amy always did enjoy pottering about with her stupid plants.

"See, it's still there as we left it. But maybe she filled the hole in when she got out or somethin'. So neighbours didn't get suspicious."

"Then let's dig it back up then."

They entered the shed and found a shovel propped up against a wall and took it out. Richard went first. It hadn't rained for a few days now so the ground was hard. After just a few minutes, he handed the shovel to Donald, sweating profusely. Donald being the strongest of the two and no doubt adrenaline and rage running through him like a mad thing, wasted no time. But after a few minutes, Richard told him to stop.

"We never dug that deep. No way. She was barely below the surface. I'm tellin' ya, she's come back from the fuckin' grave. She's a fuckin' ghoul or somethin'.

"Fuck. So what do we do? What about Kate?"

Good point. What did they do about Kate? If they phoned the police—and Richard still had to go give his statement—they would both be arrested for sure.

"Listen, I know it's hard, but we put Kate somewhere. For now. I gotta go give my fuckin' statement. We can't phone and tell them there's been another. They'll think we're involved and somehow, they might connect us to Amy. We put Kate's body in your shed for now. Until we find out where the fuck Amy is."

"How do you know she's not indoors? She could be watching us right now."

Another good point. Armed with more gardening tools, one of which was the garden fork that Amy had used to kill Brian, they searched the house. Nothing.

"Right," said Richard. "We hide Kate, clean up the mess, I

go give my statement, then tonight we wait together for Amy to come for us. I got a gun at home, that'll fuckin do it."

Donald agreed, knowing he had little choice in the matter. Tonight, this was going to end. Even if Richard had to saw Amy up into little pieces, she was going to die properly. Like she should have done in the first place.

TWELVE

She couldn't wait any longer. She desperately needed to see her baby again, know that she was safe, and that soon, very soon, Amy would be coming to take her home again. Amy took a moment to water her new plant pots —she had, after all, spent a lot of time and care to make sure they blossomed perfectly—and grabbed all her tools required to finish the job. She had wanted to make Richard's final moments painful, see him suffer as much as she had, perhaps even beg for his life, although this, knowing him, was unlikely. He wouldn't give her the satisfaction. Still, if she could look into his eyes as he stopped breathing, going to hell knowing that she had beaten him, would be enough. She put the strap-on in the rucksack and headed to Richard's house.

Amy had seen and heard pretty much everything when Richard and Donald dug up her garden and checked the house for her. She had first been watching from the bathroom window then hiding under the bed, so she knew there was a good chance she might be up against them both but this didn't deter her either. It would be good to see them die together. She could tell Donald how Kate had squirmed and screamed like a little baby as she fucked her mouth with the sex toy. Stupid fucking hippies.

It was dark when she arrived which was perfect. She could see a light on in the living room giving away their location but not hers. She crept on all fours into the front garden so they wouldn't see her from the living room and dared to peer in to see if they were together. Richard never did close his curtains completely, saying he liked to be able to see who was knocking on his door before answering. She could see someone sprawled on the sofa and knew exactly who it was. Perfect. Amy crept back outside the garden and headed around the back knowing full well the back door would be unlocked as well.

Where the other one was she didn't know and didn't care. Her knife was sharp enough for both of them and she was turning into a right little mean bitch when it came to killing people. She wondered if she could perhaps become a hired killer or something when she finished in this town. Hired to kill or hurt cheating husbands and boyfriends. Amy had an idea there was a big call for that kind of work. *Strap-on Services*. Had a nice ring to it. She couldn't hear talking or moving about upstairs so assumed the other was either out buying beer or dope or in the shower even. Assuming either of them even bothered to shower anymore. The worrying thing was that she couldn't hear Sam but the girl was probably in bed by now—a good thing, she wouldn't hear the commotion. And there was going to be a lot of commotion. Richard was going to scream liked he'd never screamed before.

She wondered how to go about it now that she was here. He was an arsehole like all the rest of them. No man could ever be trusted she had come to learn. Feeling the strap-on slide effort-lessly and seamlessly into Richard's arse would give her consid-erable pleasure. Fuck, maybe he'd even like it himself. Wouldn't surprise her. So yeah, maybe she'd make him strip off, get a good dollop of Vaseline on the toy and show him what it was like to be fucked good and proper. But that would have to come afterwards. With the fucker lying on the sofa he would have to be subdued somehow first, and she knew from listening to them there was a gun in the house. A certain element of surprise was required here.

As Kate had been, he would be stoned as well so that gave her the upper hand she needed. She could smell the rich aroma of the weed throughout the house, as though the oxygen in this place was composed of it. She pulled the knife from her rucksack and crept towards the living room door. She could hear him chuckling to himself. A stupid schoolboy chuckle that made her sick. What right did he have to laugh ever again after what he did?

Without giving it a second thought, Amy walked straight into the living room and plunged the knife into Donald's face, going straight through one cheek and coming out the other side, splitting his mouth open.

"Hi, Donald. Miss me?"

He didn't have a chance to react. Before he was even aware of her presence the knife was in his face. He jerked violently, raised his hands to remove the knife then evidently thought better of it. He turned to face her looking as though he was wearing the largest brace in history, eyes wild, blood flowing copiously down his chin.

She removed the knife taking with it the man's lips and several teeth, plus a large portion of his tongue. Donald tried to scream but could only manage a gargle as the blood rapidly filled his throat. Before the adrenaline kicked in and he could attempt to retaliate, she kicked him onto his side, quickly brought out the duct tape and tied his wrists behind his back, then his ankles. Donald appeared to be in shock still, shaking violently, eyes seeing everything and nothing as they roved around the room.

As with Brian, Amy had absolutely no desire to see

Donald's hairy arse so left the strap-on in the rucksack. It was hard work cleaning it anyway.

"So, Donald, you didn't answer my question, are you pleased to see me or not? Where's Richard by the way?"

Now that he was turned on his side he at least wasn't going to choke to death on his own blood but he still looked in bad condition, eyes rolling in his head, looking lost, the skin on his face that wasn't covered in crimson a very pallid colour. He looked like a vampire after lunch with all that running down his chin.

"Maybe I should sit and wait for Richard to come home then. You can watch me kill him."

It only then occurred to her, with her own adrenaline running through her body that if Richard wasn't here—because surely he would have heard Donald's choking and gargling and Amy's voice—she could go upstairs and at least check to see Sam was okay. Just a peek in the bedroom, careful not to wake her so she saw all this. With the knife in her hand, ready to attack Richard if necessary, she ran upstairs and checked all the bedrooms. She almost gave up until she glanced into the last one. It was dark in there but she thought she could make out a small bundle under the blanket and hear soft snoring. She was okay then. Amy wanted to go over to her, whisper in her ear that she loved her and to be strong, just for one more day, but she couldn't. If Sam woke up and stumbled downstairs it would be all over—she'd never understand. Smiling and sobbing at the same time, Amy closed the door and headed back downstairs.

In the few seconds she had taken to check on Sam, it seemed Donald hadn't wasted any time. And that perhaps he wasn't as badly injured as what he looked. Now, instead of lying sprawled on the sofa, he was on the floor trying to squirm his way over to the landline next to a coffee table. His eyes widened again when Amy walked in, trying to say something at the same time, yet incapable. His cheeks flapped when he opened his mouth like pages in a book.

"Well, look at you, all in a hurry to get somewhere. Gonna try and phone the police, were you? Let's do something about that, shall we?"

Amy straddled him and toyed with the tip of the blade around his eyeballs, as though tickling him. She remembered about pouring bleach into Kate's eyes and wished she thought of bringing more. Maybe something else, then? And just to make sure he didn't try anything clever, she picked up the loose flap of flesh that used to be his left cheek and sliced it completely off, leaving a large hole in his face, showing that side of his jaw. She did the same with the other, held them up contemplating them as though interesting artifacts she'd just discovered, then threw them away. They landed with a wet slap. It was quite funny seeing the big holes in his face and his big, fat nose in the middle, now looking completely out of place—an alien contraption. Donald also looked like he was grinning a big, skeletal grin showing off his jawbones with all his yellow teeth and this made her giggle.

Donald didn't seem to find it very funny though and resumed squirming and groaning, the veins in his neck like taut rope.

"Wait there, Donald. Just want to go find something, back in a bit."

She stood up and headed off to the kitchen, not wanting to waste any time in case Richard came back. She also didn't want Sam waking up and seeing this so would have to hide him somewhere. But that was for afterwards.

She remembered once when her sink blocked. She didn't have the money for a plumber or the knowhow to do it herself, until a friend told her to buy a bottle of caustic soda from the supermarket. Pour hot water down the sink then add a good amount and you'll see, she had said. And it had worked perfectly. The soda ate everything that had caused the blockage. She wondered now if Richard would have anything similar lying about. It would be interesting to see what it did to Donald's eyeballs. Unfortunately, though, she couldn't find anything, and time was running out. Richard could be back at any second and catch her unawares. Starting to get a little nervous, she almost gave up when her eye caught on something and she squealed in delight. She did a little preparation and hurried back.

Again, Donald, in his prolonged agony and shock had somehow managed to drag himself a little closer to the phone. How he was going to talk to the police without a mouth and a stub of a tongue she didn't know and probably neither did he. She straddled him with her concoction and froze when she heard noises outside. It sounded like someone slamming shut a garden gate. Amy jumped up and ran to the window then breathed a sigh of relief when she saw it was a neighbour returning home and staggering down the garden path. It reminded her that she needed to be quick.

She straddled Donald again, barely able to whimper by now.

"Soon be over, Donald, you can go join your slut of a wife in hell. Did you know she begged to be put out of her misery? Sobbed her little eyes out she did, so I poured bleach in them. That was fun; you should have heard her scream!"

Donald appeared to be looking at her but straight through her, almost dead from blood loss so she wasted no time. She poured half the contents of the caustic soda bottle into his gaping mouth and the rest into his eyes after cutting off his eyelids. Then she slowly poured the jug of boiling water onto it.

The response was instant. His mouth and eyeballs began to froth and sizzle as though it was boiling fat she'd poured on there. It bubbled, like an Alka-Seltzer in a glass of water. Donald went into a fit, flapping around on the floor, buckling and almost throwing Amy off, but she held on firm, fascinated as the soda burnt away into his face. His eyeballs melted, now a soft gooey substance like candlewax or bubble-gum. A weird gargling, frothing sound came from his throat and then it was gone, the soda deep inside Donald's face and throat. She wished she'd thought of this before—it would have saved her some trouble later—but even so, once she was happy the man was dead—or not, didn't matter to her—she began to saw through his neck again and as soon as his head was in her rucksack she made a hasty retreat after dragging his body out of sight and mopping up the blood as best she could.

"See you soon, Sam," she called softly. "I'll be back for you."

She cried on her way home.

THIRTEEN

She cried herself to sleep that night too. So close to her baby daughter, the most important thing in her life. The only thing in her life and she had been prevented from going to her because others had deemed it impossible for her just yet. So close, yet so far. Within arm's reach. Almost at the finishing line. She had wanted to curl up in bed beside her, sing her one of her favourite nursery rhymes, stroke her long, blonde hair and whisper in her ear how much she loved her. That from now on everything was going to be okay. But just as she promised herself last night in bed, so she told herself as she sat sipping coffee in the kitchen the next morning. Soon, so soon.

Amy guessed that Richard would probably have found Donald's body by now yet if she had heard right, he might not be so inclined to go to the police. They would consider him a suspect already, she imagined, and once Kate's body was discovered as well, he would be an even bigger suspect. And he could hardly tell them who he believed the killer to be. Maybe he'd done the same to Kate and Donald as they did to her—bury them. He'd be quite the expert by now. But all this was irrelevant right now. Brian, Jenny, Kate and Donald were history. Yesterday's news. What mattered was tomorrow's news. And the name on the headlines would be that of Richard Lenover. She didn't even care about her fat ex-boss anymore; she just wanted this over with so she could go collect Sam.

But today was not that day. As much as she wanted to, Richard would be on his guard especially once he found Donald's body and while he was under scrutiny by detectives there was little chance of him coming looking for her, so best to stay lowkey herself as well. Detectives might even be carrying out surveillance on him and his house, and that was the last thing she needed. The saddest part, thinking about all that, was that no one was looking for *her*. She could go weeks without speaking to her mum, the only real friends she had had tried to kill her so as far as the world was concerned, everything in Amy's life was fine. Nothing to report. She never even had concerned neighbours to think about. So today she was going to spend it pottering about in the garden. Maybe take some photos; who knows, seeing how creative she had been she could even win some prize. A few hundred in prize money would be a real help right now; the money she'd had in the bank had all been withdrawn and was nearly gone. Richard had a good stash and she thought she knew where he kept it, so hopefully that minor issue would be taken care of soon as well and she and Sam could get out of here.

Amy finished breakfast, washed the dishes, and looked out the window. A nice, sunny day, perfect. In the fridge was Donald's head, so she took it out and put it in the sink. That caustic soda had done a real good job, saving her a lot of messy work, especially where his throat was concerned. That stuff had burned away much of the flesh and tendons so it shouldn't take her so long this time. She turned the head upside down then opened one of the drawers and pulled out her electric knife, a wonderful invention surely designed for such things as this.

Amy plugged it in and inserted it into Donald's head then began to saw through what remained of the flesh around the exposed jaw. She'd come to learn it really smelled bad after a few days if she didn't, although having said that, she did like to leave the skin on the face. It helped remind her who she was and what she had been through. Once the flesh was cleaned out from the throat area, she took the head to the shed at the bottom of the garden where her power tools were. Being a tomboy most of her life had had its bonuses—she had more experience than most women when it came to handling such tools.

She took out the grinder, plugged it in, then sawed the top of Donald's skull off. She had to admit that now, with the empty sockets, just dried lumps of white goo sitting there instead of his eyeballs, and most of Donald's face missing, it looked pretty creepy. She hoped it wouldn't scare off the birds. Once she was finished she took it outside and gently laid it next to the other three on the makeshift shelf she'd built especially for this purpose. Now the three of them were together, one more to go. The skin had turned leathery in the sun, much like ancient Egyptian mummies, and their eyeballs Amy had had to cut out herself but using them as flowerpots had been a stroke of genius she thought. In all three heads, a cactus rose from their open skulls, reaching for the stars with their deadly prickles a warning to anything that might want to approach too close. Amy carefully inserted the next cactus plant in Donald's skull, filled it with soil then stepped back to admire her handiwork.

It really was very pretty, Sam might not think so but she didn't need to know they belonged to real people. And besides, they were unrecognisable now anyway. Bugs had managed to find a way into their open mouths and crawled around their nostrils as well. Amy chuckled. It had been them the ones to be eaten by worms and bugs, not her, after all. When it came to bringing Richard's, this would be the perfect ending to a terrible chain of events. All five left to rot and whither in the sun while she and Sam left to start a new life for themselves.

Things were going to be good again. Better than ever. Fuck Richard and his cronies and Northgate Hospital for the Mentally Impaired. Maybe she should burn the place down as well, she wondered as an afterthought. All that time cooped up in the place when she should have been at home with her baby Sam.

"Don't you worry, Sam," she muttered. "We will be together again tomorrow."

As she headed back inside, a crow flew over her garden. Perhaps by fate or coincidence, it decided in that very moment to unload its bowels. A splatter landed directly on Donald's face and ran down his bulbous nose. Amy laughed so hard she was crying when she stepped inside.

Fourteen

my listened as the journalist on the TV reported the horrific discoveries of Brian and Jenny, failing to mention the details of their deaths, only that they had been found brutally mutilated. The journalist sure as hell didn't mention they had been decapitated. What he did say though, and was more interesting to Amy, was that they had no suspects and no clues, so if anyone had any information, to please come forward. To Amy, this meant that either the police didn't consider Richard to be a suspect or they were secretly withholding that information so as not to scare him off. Amy guessed the first possibility was the most likely. The time of death would probably have been determined by now and Richard would have an alibi. It didn't mean the police were not watching Richard but Amy thought there was a good chance they wouldn't be watching him all night. Which also meant tonight was as good a time as any to finish this whole thing off.

Now that it had come to it, she was nervous as hell. She'd already thrown up in the toilet twice just thinking about the possible outcomes. Richard is ready and waiting for her and kills her before she can react, and right in front of Sam. The police catch her while she is cutting Richard's head off; off to prison forever and goodbye Sam. Sam comes in and catches her cutting Richard's head off—goodbye Sam. The risks and possibilities were endless, but the love she held in her heart for her daughter meant she had to go through with it regardless. If she didn't, it might be Richard turning the tables on her—shooting her in the head while she slept one night. Nope, it was now or never.

She picked up her rucksack, checked to ensure she had the right tools, plus one or two extras she'd thought of and made her way to Richard's home. But just before leaving, she watered her new flowerpots, just in case. It might be the last time. Amy waved goodbye to them and left.

For all she knew Richard wasn't even home and it would be a complete waste of time. He could be down the pub bragging about being a suspect in the deaths of Brian and Jenny. He wouldn't say anything about Donald or Kate though because then questions would be asked which might lead back to Amy. But all her worries were gone when she saw the light on in the living room. The only problem now was where was Sam? She would have to take her chances and hope that Sam was in bed asleep. It was late, after all. Amy went around to the back of the house and quietly let herself in, her knife gripped tightly in her hand.

The TV was on, the sound down low and she could hear loud snoring as well. It reminded Amy of a pig grunting. One with a bad cold perhaps. As she crept closer, she saw the empty beer cans strewn haphazardly about, an almost empty bottle of whiskey on the table. So he had got drunk and fallen asleep. This was just too perfect. She couldn't have asked for a better setup. All day she had been considering how his final moments should be; needles in his eyeballs, so he could know how she felt as the soil entered her own eyes while being buried alive; tape his mouth and nostrils with duct tape and let him suffocate, but bringing him back from death before he breathed his last; she was a welder, she could wrap his cock in aluminium and weld that to something. *Let's see you fuck someone over now.* The best though would be to administer a paralysing agent then slowly but surely chop him up into little pieces. He would feel everything but be unable to do anything about it. She could start with his toes, then work her way up until nothing remained but his head and torso. Cut out his tongue and even let him live, maybe. Let him suffer the rest of his life until he killed himself. But no, she had promised herself she wanted his last ever view to be of her as she watched him die, see the look of horror in his eyes just as he had seen hers. Plus the agony. So much agony.

Amy stepped into the living room, saw Richard sprawled on the sofa fast asleep and held the blade to his throat.

"Hello, Richard. Miss me?"

But then something happened she hadn't counted on. Before she even had time to drag the blade across his throat, a hand was clutching her wrist tightly, forcing her to drop the knife. Richard had been waiting for her, pretending to be asleep.

FIFTEEN

Before Amy could react, Richard jumped up and punched her on the nose. It exploded showering her in crimson, white-hot agony like a bolt of lightning shooting up her face. She screamed, both in pain and horror for allowing herself to be so easily tricked. It was over.

"Think you was gonna cut my head off as well, did ya, you sick bitch? Think I'm fuckin' stupid? You shoulda stayed where you were, would've been so much easier for everyone. Now look what you've done."

"You bastard! You buried me alive, you fucker! Where's Sam? Tell me where my baby is?"

She spat blood out at Richard when she spoke, as it poured from her broken nose, but now she was barely aware. All that mattered was seeing her daughter for the last time before Richard surely killed her. Again.

"You just won't give up, will ya? How many fuckin' times we gotta go through this before it enters your thick head? You shoulda stayed buried, Amy. That, or we never shoulda let them release you from hospital. I guess it's my fault, thinkin' you was better. Too late now though. I can't let you do to me what you did to them. You gotta die for good, Amy."

"Just let me see my baby!" she screamed. "I want to see her first. You tell me where she is!"

Richard sighed and drew his fist back to punch her again. He was going to bludgeon her to death, she could see it. Once he started, there was no stopping him.

"Honestly, I hope you two meet up again and sort things out. She didn't deserve none of this. I'll tell you for the last time, Amy. Sam—"

But he didn't get the chance. Richard might be stronger than her, but he was also stupid. Stupid and half drunk which made what Amy did next much easier. It must never have crossed his mind she might be carrying another knife, but she was, in her back pocket. She quickly grabbed it and stabbed him in the eye. She thought of burying the blade up the handle then decided against it. She pulled it out.

The eyeball came with it, perched on the tip of the blade like a morsel, nerves dangling like spaghetti. Amy brought it closer to her, almost tempted to nibble on it, see what it tasted like. She chose not to. Richard sunk to his knees, howling and screaming, his one remaining eye focused on the other stuck to the tip of the knife. She thought of making him eat it instead. He was making a lot of noise which might wake Sam, though, so she kicked him onto his back and quickly pulled out the duct tape, taping his mouth. Then she did the same to his wrists behind his back, then his ankles. She was taking no chances.

Now, seeing him lying there, all the rage and anger that had been building up threatened to overwhelm her. Her hands were shaking, tears running down her face and mingling with the sticky blood from a still-throbbing nose. So many things she wanted to do to him, see him cry and squeal in utter agony, and he was going to do just that, but all the right tools she had back at home in her shed. If she could get him there safely...

For that he would have to be further subdued. A missing eyeball and a bit of duct tape might not be enough to see him escape somehow, alert the neighbours or something. She had just the thing to keep him quiet while she led him home.

Amy opened her rucksack and brought out the little tube. Richard was still groaning and whimpering, so she straddled him and tore off the tape. Before he could say anything, she pinched his lips together and emptied the superglue onto them, leaving just enough to fill one nostril. Just so he had an idea of what it was like to suffocate slowly. She waited a few minutes until it was completely dry then stood up. As an afterthought, so he couldn't use his remaining eye to search for help, she brought out the other tube and covered his eyelid in more glue, sealing his eye shut.

"There, that should keep you quiet for a while. C'mon, up you get."

It was a good job Richard was thin, she thought as she struggled to get him to his feet. He moaned and tried to resist but now he was completely blind, no idea where to go and incapable of moving anyway. It was also a good thing Amy lived just ten minutes away.

"Be back soon, Sam," she whispered. She grabbed her rucksack and led Richard to her place, gripping his arm tightly all the way and letting him know there was a knife at his throat. Blind, he didn't resist.

Once home, she led him to the living room and let him drop to the floor. There was absolutely no way he was going anywhere so she left him there and headed to the garden shed where she kept her tools. She had built up quite the collection of power tools over the years and it was tough to decide which ones to use. But really, after debating for a few minutes it was quite obvious. Richard needed to understand what he had done. He had left Amy to die slowly so surely he must do the same. She grabbed what she needed and returned to the living room.

He was groaning and whimpering still in there, rolling around like a big, fat maggot which she thought kind of summed him perfectly. "It must be terrible, barely able to breathe, blind, immobile. Just like being buried, right?"

With his bound feet he tried to kick out at her.

"No one knows you're here, Dick. If I died, you'd starve to death. Although that might not be so bad considering."

She really wanted to hear his suffering, so she grabbed her knife and was about to slice through the glue so he could talk again, then thought better of it. She cut off his lips instead, then, carefully, because she also wanted to look in his one remaining eye as she got to work on him, cut off his glued eyelid. Now he could watch perfectly. Amy waited for him to stop screaming, then wiped the blood from his mouth so he didn't choke to death.

"There, that better? Got anything to say? You took my Sam from me again, Dick. I can't let you get away with that. I hope you've been treating her well, or I'll kill all your friends as well. The ones that are left, that is."

She knew that Richard had quite a threshold when it came to withstanding pain—she'd seen him take some pretty severe beatings when he was drunk—so it wasn't much of a surprise when he tried to sit up and talk to her. At first, all he could manage was to drool and spit saliva at her but what he said to her was the last thing she had expected.

"Amy, listen to me. You're makin' a big mistake. Sam is dead. You killed her."

"Bullshit! Don't you say that! She's back home asleep."

"Kill me if you want, I don't care, but you gotta listen. You remember bein' in Northgate?"

"Yes."

"You were admitted three times over the years. They took your pillow away, you remember why?"

"Because...because I was suicidal. I tried to suffocate myself."

"Think, Amy. What else did you do with the pillow?"

Amy sat back. All thoughts of torturing Richard right now forgotten. An image flashed past. Of her straddling someone on a bed. Crying and howling for what seemed like hours until she could take it no more. Then the crying stopped. The image disappeared. Amy shook her head, as if by doing so another recollection might return. There was something in the peripheral of her mind, trying to poke through but she wouldn't let it. Couldn't let it.

"No. No, I don't want to talk about that. You shut up or I'll cut your tongue out."

"You killed Sam, Amy. Smothered her with the pillow. Because you had a hangover and she wouldn't shut up. Then you took her into the garden and buried her."

"Shut up! That's bullshit! Sam is alive! She's at home, safe and sound in bed!"

Another image flashed past. Of carrying a tiny bundle to the garden, a small hole there. Her beloved garden where she spent most of her time. Then the image changed to the hole having been filled in, there were people in the garden with her. Richard was there. Jenny, Brian, others. They were screaming something at her. She shook her head, then looked up at Richard, glaring at her with his one remaining eye.

"A few days went past. You kept askin' us where Sam was. Then later that day you asked me to marry you."

"Wait, no! You asked *me* to marry you. I said no, so you told your friends all that crap about me. Told them I'd been flirting with Donald and others, so you fucking buried me. You took Sam with you."

"When I said no, you told me what you'd done to Sam.

First, ya said she was at ya mother's house, then you took me and the others you've since killed into the garden and dug her up, showed us her body. Then ya went totally fuckin' nuts. We kept it a secret but had you admitted to Northgate.

"After a couple of weeks you stopped askin' for Sam so they let you out. But you kept havin' fuckin' breakdowns, demandin' to know where she was. You thought we'd kidnapped her. So back to Northgate you went."

Amy slumped against the sofa, tears were running down her face but she was barely aware. It was a lie, it had to be. He was trying to talk his way out of being tortured to death like the others. She had been hiding in the wardrobe when she heard Richard telling Jenny about Amy flirting with Donald. How he had proposed to her and she'd had rejected him. Hadn't she? If so, why was there a window in the wardrobe? With steel bars on it? It didn't make sense. Nothing did. Yes, she had been in Northgate a few times but that was because they had taken Sam from her and wouldn't let Amy see her. And then when she was released for the third time, she had overheard them planning on killing her. So Richard could keep Sam for himself.

"I've told ya so many times, Amy. We all tried to tell ya, but ya wouldn't accept what ya did. She's buried there now, go take a look."

"No, that's wrong. *I* was buried there. *You* all buried me in there. You can't say I'm making that up!"

"We showed ya Sam's body again, told ya what you did. Ya said ya wanted to be buried with her. That if we didn't you'd kill us all. Ya even tried to fuckin stab me, in front of the others. So we gave up. We put somethin' in your drink to knock ya with but obviously it wasn't enough, and ya managed to dig your way out. That's why, Amy. You could ask the others but ya fuckin' killed 'em like ya said ya would."

There had been something in the hole with her. Something

hard. But hadn't that been the dildos they'd rammed up her? She couldn't remember now.

"Where are her clothes? Toys? Photos? You thought of that? We threw everythin' away so ya wouldn't keep thinkin' about her but it didn't work either."

Yes, that was true. Now that she thought about it, there was nothing here to suggest Sam had even existed. Only in her mind. Buried.

"Listen, just fuckin' kill me if you're gonna 'cause I'm sick of this shit. Ya killed our daughter and can't fuckin' handle the consequences, so either kill me or let me go."

Amy looked up, not quite sure what she just heard. He was still blaming her for all this? Sitting there with half his face missing and one eye and still had the audacity to blame her for Sam's death? He was practically begging her to kill him just so he didn't have to listen to her anymore. Okay, that was fine with her. Absolutely fine. But it wasn't going to be fast. All this talk of burying gave her an idea.

Amy went outside to the back garden and turned on the lights that lit everything up. From the shed, she grabbed the shovel and dug a new hole. It took a while but the rage coursing through her gave her the extra strength to get the job done. When she thought it was deep enough she went back inside. Richard remained where he was immobile but in that solitary eye she saw fear for the first time.

"You wanna die, you're gonna die. But on my terms."

She fired up the oxyacetylene torch. Richard tried to struggle, squirming on the floor like all the others had done. With her knife, she cut away his clothes until he was naked, his flaccid little cock like a shrivelled grape. Then she directed the white-hot flame onto his balls and left it there until the sack popped and colourless secretions dribbled out then melted, as did his cock while Richard howled like some demonic creature in utter agony.

That was just for starters.

Amy turned off the equipment and dragged him outside. She had a roll of barbed wire there that she had been planning on using at some point but had a better use for it now. She opened it up then dragged Richard onto it and rolled him over until he was neatly wrapped up. She kicked him a few times to make sure it really stuck to him good. Then, with just his head sticking out of the barbed wire, she dragged him to the hole and kicked him in, filling the soil again until just his head poked out of the ground.

"You buried me and my baby so I think it's only fitting I do the same to you. What do you think, Dick?"

"You're a sick fuckin' bitch, that's what. And if hell exists that's where ya goin'."

"Oh, I've been in hell for years. Ever since I met you."

Amy returned inside and came back out with her equipment. The flame sparked into life. She squatted beside him and looked into his remaining eyeball.

"This is gonna hurt, Dick. A lot, I'm afraid. Well, actually, I'm not afraid, 'cause you deserve this, but know that when I finish I'm going to get Sam and we're going to live happily ever after. How does that sound?"

"You fuckin' mad, sick fu—"

Amy directed the flame at his face.

Again, it was a warm night, with barely any breeze so the stench of burning hair and flesh was immediate and wafted up Amy nostrils like a thick smog. And the effects of the flame on his face was immediate too. It sizzled like frying bacon then gradually began to melt from his face while he screamed and shook his head from side to side. In doing so, bits of flesh were sent flying, some landing on Amy's face like sticky boogers.

She directed the flame all over his face rather than in one spot so that it melted as one, like a rubber mask. His remaining eyeball popped and spat out pus and thick secretions. His nose was reduced to a dripping stub that dropped off leaving a large hole in the middle of his face. Other holes appeared in his cheeks, his forehead until what looked like a crazed skull grinning back at her, little lumps of flesh like confetti stuck there, stubbornly refusing to budge.

His tongue melted in his open mouth and dribbled down the back of his throat, his hair all gone now, yet still his head thrashed from side to side, even when the flesh was completely burnt off. Amy gagged a couple of times from the smell, reminiscent of burnt pork. Finally, Richard's head stopped thrashing and was still. Wisps of smoke drifted from his skull like fleeing spectres, empty sockets like craters still filled with some sticky substance. Amy smiled. She wasn't finished yet though.

She went to the shed and took out an axe then in one deft swing, sliced off his head as though swinging at a golf ball. It rolled to the bottom of the garden. She covered the remaining soil where his neck still showed then picked up the skull and took it inside the shed. Then, she plugged in the grinder and deftly cut through the top. Next to the other flowerpots it sat, at odds with them, the only one with no flesh left on it, even though the flesh on the others was starting to peel off. Amy poured in a little soil, collected the last cactus plant she had and neatly sat it in the middle of Richard's skull.

"There, ain't that cute! All together again like in the old times!"

There was just one thing left to do. Amy headed back inside and grabbed the bottle of red wine she had bought especially for the occasion. She opened it and took it back outside, leaving it next to a couple of deckchairs beside the flowerpots. Sitting down, she poured herself a glass, took a sip and contemplated her new garden and the life she was going to be leading soon. She finished her wine, was about to refill it when she had another idea.

The doctors had spoken of repressed memories. What they should have spoken about were buried memories. She had buried her daughter in her garden, they said, then her brain had buried the incident deep within her subconscious so she could cope with what she had done. But, of course, memories never truly stay buried forever. Always lurking like a bad dream to come back and haunt you. And sometimes they were misleading and jumbled, mixing truths with half lies. She knew that now. Her memories had become confusing, and she had been incapable of telling fact from fiction. But not anymore.

She set down her glass and returned to the shed, then brought out a shovel. There, right where they had buried her she began digging. It didn't take long before the shovel connected with something hard lying in the soil. She set down the shovel, gently picked up the delicate bundle and took it back to where the deckchairs were. Then, she unwrapped it and set Sam down in the chair next to hers.

"There you go. That's better, isn't it, Sam. We're like a proper family again."

"Sure, Mum! Love you!"

"No one will ever try to take you from me and no one can hurt us anymore."

We're going to live happily ever after!"

Acknowledgments

Some stories I can remember the exact time and place where the original idea came from. More often than not, it's when I'm in bed watching some shitty movie and bored and my mind starts wandering. With Buried, however, I have not the slightest idea how it came about. Can't remember a thing. All I do remember is something about a cactus plant. Do not ask what movie I was watching that night—must have been good.

The rest I probably spent a few days thinking about until I had enough material to write the story you've just read. So with that revelation out of the way, all that remains, as always, is to thank those that helped me put it together to something vaguely publishable.

First, Horrorsmith Publishing for the formatting. Great job as always. BetiBup for the cover, and most importantly of all, my ARC team who gave me some great feedback and picked out all those pesky plot holes and typos. In no special order, Ali Sweet, Carol Howley, Derek Thomas, Shannon Ettaro, Corrina Morse (No Remorse Reviews), Margaret Hamnett, Kate DeJonge, Jennifer Bauter, Heather Larson, Fallon Raynes, Donna Latham, Kristen LeAnn, Jessica Shelly, Samantha Hawkins, Molly Squires, Anja Henriksen, Leah Dawn Baker, Shannon Zablocki. Thank you all as always—you're the best!

ALSO BY JUSTIN BOOTE

Man's Best Friend—an extreme novella

Love You to Bits—an extreme novella

(Both available on Godless and Amazon)

Short Story Collections:

Love Wanes, Fear is Forever

Love Wanes, Fear is Forever: Volume 2

Love Wanes, Fear is Forever: Volume 3

Novels:

Serial

Combustion

Carnivore: Book 1 of The Ghosts of Northgate trilogy

The Ghosts of Northgate: Book 2 of The Ghosts of Northgate trilogy

A Mad World: Book 3 of The Ghosts of Northgate trilogy

Short stories available on Godless:

Badass

Grandma Drinks Blood

A Question of Possession

If Flies Could Fart

About the Author

Justin Boote is an Englishman living in Barcelona for nearly thirty years and has been writing horror and dark fiction for approximately 6 years. He spent the first 4 years writing short stories, having around fifty published in a variety of magazines and anthologies before turning his attention to novels. To date he has self- published four short stories, three short story collections, four novels, and a five-book demon/zombie series, The Undead Possession series. He lives with his wife, son, and cat and when he is not writing he is usually thinking about writing, playing Candy Crush, or feeding Fat Cat.

He can be found at his Facebook group https://www.face book.com/groups/457222379195724

And his website

https://justinboote.com/

Printed in Great Britain
by Amazon

45855201R00059